RAIN OVER MADRID

RAIN OVER MADRID

ANDRÉS BARBA

Translated from the Spanish by
Lisa Dillman

Hispabooks
Publishing

Hispabooks Publishing, S. L.
Madrid, Spain
www.hispabooks.com

Originally published in Spain as *Ha dejado de llover* by Anagrama, 2012
First published in English by Hispabooks, 2014
English translation copyright © by Lisa Dillman
Design © Simonpates - www.patesy.com

A CIP record for this book is available from the British Library

ISBN 978-84-942284-7-6 (trade paperback)
ISBN 978-84-942284-8-3 (ebook)
Legal Deposit: M-14896-2014

To Carmen M. Cáceres,
may we always
be young and unwise together

To Simón,
because it's true that behind
every great woman is always a great cat

CONTENTS

FATHERHOOD

Whenever people at get-togethers started talking about their childhoods, he almost invariably told the same story: the one about the day his mother took him, age seven, to a casting call for the *Sesame Street Encyclopedia* TV commercial. He'd been an exceptionally good-looking child, and even now, more than twenty-five years later, some of his childhood photos astonished him, actually produced something akin to anguish, as though a beautiful child—particularly a child who had once been *him*—were a premonition, the sign of something fearsome. His mother's ferocious pride at her son's good looks had been the source of at least a dozen droll anecdotes, and the one about the *Sesame Street Encyclopedia* casting call had the additional quality, for those who could see it, of allowing insights into a large part of his childhood. And he liked that. By and large, when he told the story, he would describe the mothers first; he would endow each of them with some minor detail or distinguishing trait of his own mother. Dolled up and buxom as hens, they all exhibited some characteristic of hers: one had a grating, derisive cackle; another stood haughty and silent; another—more pragmatic—chatted away in an attempt to be pleasant, praising the good looks of whichever child stood before her, so as to immediately win over a devoted interlocutor; another stood stiff and nervous, her huge, sweaty hand in his. He'd draw out the story, noting that he'd been having stomach trouble for two weeks, that in fact he was *still having* stomach trouble the day of the casting call. Two weeks of near-constant trips to the bathroom had left his skin with a sallow, olive tone. As a kid—he'd go on, to insure everyone got the point of the story—he had markedly almond-shaped eyes. Usually, after a casting call (at that one, they'd had to sing in little choruses of three, "*All the letters, A to Z, come have fun and read with me*," while standing before a table where five adults with an air of unconcealed contempt sat jotting notes), the kids would wait with some of the mothers, who'd be more nervous than ever. That day, he knew he was going to be chosen, because as he was getting ready to leave, he'd overheard a comment.

"The Oriental boy is perfect."

What good would it have done to explain that his supposed Orientalism was in fact just gastroenteritis? He recalled his mother's jitters when they left and the man's surprise on asking his name, assuming he was going to hear an Asian surname. On the way home, his mother pranced along, brimming with glee, heels clicking as she repeated over and over, "I knew it, I *knew* it . . ."

Every time she said it, she first gazed off into space, then turned to look at him, and then back off into space again, as though she needed his diminutive form to corroborate whatever it was that she seemed to glimpse beyond the enormous buildings on the Gran Vía, some vague, glimmering image, elusive even to her. He recalled the energetic and no longer sweaty squeeze of her hand in his, recalled feeling like a fraud having been chosen for being something he was not. He was afraid to confess, but his mother's joy was so inordinate and his torment so vast that at dinner that night, on the verge of tears, he finally told her, a knot in his throat.

"Mamá, they picked me because they think I'm Asian."

"Nonsense."

"That's what one of the men said."

He recalled that that was the first time his mother's avarice, a well-concealed avarice, had made itself known to him. He recalled that he'd never noticed it until then, and realizing how wrong he'd been about her made him feel he couldn't trust the rest of his beliefs or feelings, either. She stared at him fixedly for a few seconds, as though some ominous idea were crossing her mind, and then settled the matter with a simple "well if they think you're Asian, then Asian you shall be."

Again his mother seemed to reflect for a moment, taking three more contemplative spoonfuls of soup, and then, pointing her spoon at him, in an inscrutable tone that might as easily have conveyed threat as inspiration as absolute resolve, she concluded, "I assure you, you're going to be the most Asian child you've ever seen in your life."

Normally, when he told the story, he had the entire audience eating out of his hand by this point. The rest was basically a victory lap—his mother taking him to a department store to buy him a little kimono; the

11

director's bewilderment on seeing him decked out like that, how he'd shouted, right in front of his mother, *What idiot put the kid in that get-up?*; his shame at having to return to school and hear his classmates chime in unison, "*All the letters, A to Z, come have fun and read with me*". There was something cathartic about describing his own humiliation in such gleeful, carefree terms, and something phony about it, too, and he knew it. The irrefutable proof lay in the peculiar mix of bitterness and compassion he still felt for his mother all these years later, as though the woman he now saw once every three months—the woman who still lived with his aunt in the same old apartment—had been born and raised ill-prepared for everything, mistaken about everything. Her peculiar concept of *real life*, her wild and often risible ambition had meant that his entire childhood was spent cringing in embarrassment for her, and that embarrassment had later warped and morphed into detached pity and an inability to keep his cool when he saw her. His phase of blaming her for everything had ended long ago, but he hadn't been able to rid himself of the sense that everything his mother felt—including love, desire, and the urge to prosper—was so simplistic that it was inevitable that she'd never found her place in the very world she struggled so hard to leave a mark on. She was still chatty and ebullient—had been so to an almost histrionic degree during his glory days with the band—but time had taken its toll on her, too; her mouth was a bit more rough-hewn, her breath a bit more labored, her ambitions a bit more moderate. Did all of that come across in the simple *Sesame Street Encyclopedia* casting call

12

anecdote? He thought it did. Once, he'd actually told it during a radio interview, and on his way out, one of the sound techs had come up to him and told him as much.

"I can imagine what it must have been like, having a mother like that," she said.

"Bet you can't," he replied, smiling.

It began early on, almost from the start—the feeling, the sense he got that music made things solid, the strange confidence he had in his own talent, as though it were easy to see that his intelligence was naturally fleeter than that of most people around him. He spent his days composing, attending university to pass the time and to seek out others like him. They weren't hard to find. If his knack for composing was something he'd always seemed to have at his fingertips, something that had been a gift, the knack for finding whoever he was looking for was one he'd honed with confidence and ease. He formed a band that split up after only a few months because each member was convinced he was a rock-and-roll genius. Then another one that lasted a little longer, long enough to record several demos. But they split up, too. Success arrived in the most unexpected way, when he was twenty-eight and had given up on music as a commercial pursuit and formed a new band, one he just wanted to have fun with. A semi-famous director used one of their tracks as the theme song for his movie, and suddenly it was getting played all over—in several different commercials, on the radio, at almost every bar in town. He didn't get his hopes up, because he knew full well what the music business was like, but for those few years, he enjoyed his minor success like someone who'd suddenly won the lottery—by squandering it all.

"So what's it like to wake up one day and suddenly be famous?" a third-rate journalist from a women's magazine once inquired, after asking the most outrageous place he'd ever made love, his favorite spot in Madrid, and which he liked better, salty or sweet (that, in fact, was the song's title—"Sweet").

"It doesn't feel like anything, really; you're still the same old asshole you were the day before."

In giving that answer, he was aware of the fact that he was implicitly acknowledging his own fame, that his reply was imbued with the exact quality he had derided in so many other C-list celebrities interviewed by so many other women's magazines: the pretentious indulgence and oily self-satisfaction of a public swimming-pool Romeo.

Perhaps the most honest and straightforward response would simply have been to say that he wasn't famous. Only rarely did a twenty-something-year-old girl stop him on the street to ask if it was him, only rarely did anyone ask him to autograph a record. He didn't know if that was enough to be considered famous, but he did know that it had been more than enough to arouse the disdainful envy of half of Madrid's independent music scene. The first and also the most persistent corollary to his minor celebrity had been that experience of envy. It was an ugly, rancorous envy, a neurotic envy that led him to lose both friends and his temper more than once. It tended to manifest itself in veiled, dishonest ways, with insincere compliments or sometimes with comments about how interesting the music he used to make (when he had no success to speak of) was, and how uninteresting the music he made now (when he did) was, or in the even more veiled way

14

of avoiding all talk that had anything to do with what he was currently writing. His minor celebrity had other consequences, stranger and less predictable consequences, too: he felt, during that time, as though many of his desires had been extinguished. Simple, generalized desires that, once satisfied, left an aftertaste akin to humiliation, like when a child who spends all afternoon bawling for cotton candy finally gets it in his greedy little hands and instantly realizes how sticky it is, how excessively sweet it is, how having his wish granted has immediately generated other, ancillary desires: water to quench his thirst, the chance to wash his hands. It wasn't even really that desire, per se, had been stamped out, more that he got the sense that success had reduced the world to its narrowest conception, to a strange dulling of physical realities, of his views, of music, of his youth.

That was the year he met Sonia. He'd seen her at two or three of his gigs. She was a friend of a friend of someone or other. As soon as he saw her, he was pretty sure he could get her into bed without too much effort. He'd never had a lot of trouble getting the girls he wanted into bed, and it was even easier back then. The ease with which he triumphed in that arena hadn't made him vain, had instead made him almost entirely unaware of how most people's love lives worked. He wasn't selfish, but he was careless and forgetful; he paid no attention to others' feelings, but nor did he pay attention to his own. In truth, he lived in a rather numb and lonely world, emotionally speaking. He liked sex, but it only really turned him on when he was absolutely certain that he was giving someone pleasure, and his interest waned quickly, as soon as he suspected he'd really touched something in a girl, something deep and intimate. What's more, he got along better with most girls afterward. Having sex early on, as soon as possible, seemed to tear down a wall rather than build one up—he felt himself relax and felt that the girls, too, became somehow more open, more at peace. His sex life was one of overwhelming mediocrity, like an utterly unremarkable episode of kleptomania, and he had the reputation of being a Don Juan when in fact he was not.

Sonia was like all the others. Girlish and pretty, she tried not to come off as too available or eager but was entirely unsuccessful. Her beauty had something malevolent and self-conscious about it. She'd just moved out of her parents' house, now lived alone in a miniscule loft on the Calle Madera, and was five years younger than him. The first thing she'd said to him was that she loved his music but one of his most recent songs was absolutely terrible. Half an hour later, they were outside kissing, and two hours after that, he was undressing her at his place. She had a small, tight body, more hang-ups than she wanted to admit, a loveliness that was bony and fresh, and the tip of one of her nipples turned in.

"It just doesn't want to come out," she said, smiling, when he took off her bra. Sonia's technique for coping with hang-ups back then consisted of overtly stating them as quickly and as head-on as possible.

She moved boldly, as though attempting to convince herself she was an enormously sexual person, contorting too extravagantly, talking dirty in a way that seemed forced, and then falling silent, awaiting a reaction to each of her assertions, as though some object in the room might move in response.

"You have such a juicy cock."

He couldn't help laughing. When she stopped playing the nymph, he liked her more, actually. There was something categorical about her, something taut and affirmative; she was a true rebel, though he didn't know what she was rebelling against. He didn't see himself falling in love with her, but he couldn't help feeling an immediate affection for her. When he watched her up close as she slept, he sometimes became absorbed in the tiny, ordinary beauty of her face. He liked having her there, liked that she talked so much, that she pretended to be mysterious and have somewhat extravagant appetites. She was, actually, mysterious, though not in the way she intended. She skirted the topic of her family at every turn. So much so that he began to assume there was a truly dark episode buried there. When he asked her directly, she would simply say that they didn't really get along.

"Like most families," she'd conclude, making light.

Then, four months after he met her, it happened. She turned up at his place early one morning, looking like she hadn't slept much, and blurted it out in the doorway, before he'd even invited her in.

"I'm pregnant."

"Are you sure?"

"Absolutely."

"You can't be."

"Of course I can."

The start of the conversation had rattled him so much that he hadn't even stood back to let her through. He stepped aside and Sonia marched purposefully in, talking to herself.

"I can't be, he says . . ."

"Alright, relax."

"I am relaxed."

"Do you want to get an abortion?"

She had her back to him, he remembered, and at that exact moment, she whirled to face him with an entirely unfamiliar air.

"Do you think I came here to be saved by the likes of *you?*"

There was genuine disdain in Sonia's question. Her face seemed to be glowing, she wore a twisted smile. It was only an instant, a few tenths of a second, but he realized at that precise instant that no matter what they did, nothing would ever erase that expression. It bore the full weight of authenticity, and some part of Sonia had been inscribed there, indelibly. The idea of help, or love, or simple companionship didn't enter into it. Nor did the question of whether or not Sonia was going to have the child. *Of course* she was going to have it. Her *of course* contained, or so it seemed to him at the time, something that passed him over, out of shame, as though he were a half-man incapable of assuming the most obvious fundamentals of responsibility. He felt nothing, really, nothing he could express in words. The baby was still something too abstract to be conceived of, and the twenty-four-year-old Sonia—in an anxious rage—was all too concrete. He felt as though he weren't physically there, in his own living room, as though the simple objects that made up his home had become somehow incomprehensible. An hour later, he was holding her in his arms, and two weeks after that, she'd moved in. It was a nearly unilateral decision, and he put up no resistance. Sonia arrived with three suitcases, two new lamps, and a monumental urge to rearrange all of the furniture.

For several months, they played the happy couple. It was an unnatural and somewhat ludicrous game. They slept together. He would turn over and she'd spoon him from behind. They didn't talk about the baby. He couldn't remember what it was that they talked about. He did, of course, remember that there were times when he'd suddenly become aware of Sonia's presence, a strange presence that he'd inadvertently overlooked and that then became palpable once more. They went to the movies, she tagged along to concerts, and afterward she'd have a beer with the band, pretending to be the happily pregnant rocker's wife. He didn't feel tense or trapped by the situation, instead felt weightless and a bit indifferent, as though he still believed the whole thing were simply a transitory circumstance. And really, he only felt connected to her in a fraternal sort of way, through mild, conventional affection. They rarely made love. Sonia seemed no longer to need it, and he was finding it increasingly odd, as though the child—the presence of the child, a presence that was increasingly tangible—had absolved them of the obligation.

One day, as he was leaving the apartment, a man approached him.

"Are you Sonia's boyfriend?"

"Yes."

"I'm her father. Could we go get a coffee?"

He looked like a real estate developer—elegantly dressed, balding, hair slicked back, face a bit doughy but skin exhibiting the smoothness only opulence can provide—and he wore too much cologne. He pictured him as the epitome of a certain kind of Iberian male: married to a frigid blonde, eating enormous roasts every Sunday. He said that they were worried, that they knew Sonia was pregnant, that she wouldn't pick up the phone when any of them called anymore, even her siblings. He had a disturbing way of using the plural for everything he said, as though he were representing an organization rather than talking about a family. In fact, every one of the man's gestures seemed commercial, including the hand-reach he used to stop him from pulling his out wallet to pay for the coffee.

"This is on me."

He really only wanted to know if Sonia was OK, if she needed anything, if she was having any difficulties with the pregnancy. He left a card, on which he jotted a private number where he could be reached at any time, and asked him not to tell Sonia about their meeting, all with a kind of phony camaraderie that riled him, because it made him an accessory.

"So. You're . . . a musician, right?" he eventually asked, with a certain disdainful air. He recognized this gesture of Sonia's, suddenly transplanted onto the face of that man.

The first thing he did that night was to tell Sonia about it, if only to rid himself of the feeling that he'd colluded with her father. First she became irate and insisted on hearing every detail of the conversation—seeming excessively concerned about exactly what he'd told her father—and then she grew silent and pensive. Finally, she cried, alone in the bedroom. He went in and sat beside her and placed a hand on her shoulder.

"You don't have to try to be nice," she responded.

It had been an unaffected gesture, perhaps one of the few unaffected gestures he'd made toward her, so he was stung by the fact that this of all gestures was the one Sonia saw as staged. He felt deadened and strange—as though his presence were unnecessary in the world, even to touch the shoulder of this pregnant girl—but also alright. One thing would lead to another, he thought, and life would once more resume its normal course, even if he didn't know what those words meant in that particular combination, referring to life—*its normal course*. He could think of the baby only in abstract terms, regardless of the fact that Sonia's pregnancy was increasingly obvious. If all went well, it would be born in four months. Sonia remained pensive for a few more days, and then one night when they were almost ready to go to bed, she made a disturbing declaration.

"There's something I have to tell you, something I haven't told you up until now." She spoke the words with such solemnity that he immediately stopped doing the dishes and turned to face her.

"What is it?"

"I'm a millionaire."

"What do you mean, you're a millionaire?"

The declaration was so absurd that he didn't know what to think.

"Just what I said. I'm a millionaire. I have a lot of money."

"How much money are we talking about?" he asked. He found the conversation almost comical. It was comical, but, for some reason, it was also irritating him. Perhaps it was just that the ridiculousness of that word—*millionaire*—rubbed him the wrong way.

"In cash, about three hundred thousand euros, mostly in stocks, and in property, two houses in Madrid, not counting my share of my father's stuff."

"And what is *your father's stuff?*"

"A villa, two lumber mills, a furniture factory, six or seven houses, maybe more, I don't know; there're other things, but I can't remember them all right now."

He was silent for a moment. Then the only thing he could think to ask was, "So why were you living in that tiny loft when I met you?"

"I don't know, I felt like it."

"You *felt like it?*"

Sonia's reply exploded like gunfire.

"Yes, *I felt like it.*"

They spoke a little more, somewhat perfunctorily, and then went to bed. Sonia didn't spoon him that night, and the next day, he looked back on their conversation with genuine displeasure. He didn't think he had any kind of inferiority complex with regard to her money. The sum was so colossal that he had trouble even imagining it. He'd never been particularly interested in money; he'd always had enough to live on, and at that time, thanks to his minor celebrity and the tours he was doing, he had more than enough. He spent what he had as if it were burning a hole in his pocket and was vaguely disdainful of those who were frugal and meticulous with their money, as though he associated that sort of behavior with inevitable unhappiness. What really upset him about the conversation with Sonia was the lie it had involved, a lie that had been perpetuated over the course of many months. And the way Sonia related to her own wealth seemed infantile: she had demonstrated a certain degree of bad faith in acting like she didn't have all that money, in refusing to use her property—something he couldn't articulate but that irritated him and negated the possibility, by that point already rather remote, of staying with her for the rest of his life.

By chance that month, he had a series of concerts in provincial cities that kept him away from home more than usual, and when he finished the tour, he decided not to go straight back. For ten-plus days, the only news he'd had from Sonia had come in the form of a few laconic voicemails, and in the final city on his tour, he slept with a girl about twenty years old who took him back to her shared apartment. There, surrounded by photos of the girl, in that tiny bedroom, lying naked with the body of a stranger curled up on the other side of the bed, it struck him that his life for the past year, since he'd met Sonia—and maybe longer, maybe his entire life—had transpired in a way that suddenly seemed hazy and incomprehensible, as though it were nothing but an accumulation of paradoxes and more or less absurd situations. The first time he thought he was going to be a father was while staring at the girl's naked back—hunched like an old man's—and the seductive curve of her hips, and the roundness of her buttocks, which had an unusual birthmark, a little spot in the shape of Australia. He put a hand on her hip and she responded by turning to face him. She was pretty, though sleepiness and too much booze the night before had diminished her beauty. They had sex again, in a way that was slow and careful but also a bit clinical, as though the two felt engrossed but distant, and all the while, he couldn't stop thinking about Sonia, about Sonia and about the baby, and it was in that strange space of physical intimacy—in the contact with the girl's skin and the roundness of her body—that he felt it for the first time, felt that he was going to be a father in just a few months, and the mother was none other than Sonia.

When he got home, he found her working at the computer, silent and sullen. She turned and stared at him for what seemed a long time. He didn't even dare to approach, didn't dare to say hello; the distance between them was abysmal.

"This is not what I had imagined. This is not the life I want."

Two prefabricated sentences. Two sentences Sonia must have been thinking to herself for perhaps quite some time. It struck him as slightly ludicrous to have to beg forgiveness for not having lived up to expectations that he himself had never set, so he didn't do it. Nor did she demand it of him. In the brief space of that week, she'd become a different person, perhaps the one that she really was, and in order to make a decision, the person that she really was needed to feel a little disdain for him.

"I talked to my parents. I think I'm going to go home. For now. Then I'll figure out what to do later. Do you want me to let you know when the baby's born?"

"Of course I do."

"Help me take these suitcases down, I can't manage by myself."

She was a strong woman, much stronger than he was, he thought to himself at that moment, though it was the first time he'd ever had that conviction. That tiny, pregnant twenty-four-year-old who lumbered awkwardly, placing a hand on her hip, could have literally climbed over a tank right then if she'd put her mind to it. He walked her to the taxi, and as they said goodbye, he bent to give her a kiss.

"Don't even think about it," she said, slamming the door. The driver didn't dare to protest.

The baby was born two months later.

"Sonia's about to give birth," one of her brothers informed him brusquely over the phone. "At the Clínica de la Inmaculada, room 342, maternity ward. She asked me to let you know."

They'd spoken on the phone several times over the course of those months but hadn't seen each other. Sonia had been torn between the ill will she bore him and that reserved for her family. In the end, the ill will she bore him won out, and because her family shared that particular ill will, his reencounter with them was an interesting one. If he'd known the degree of animosity he was going to face at the clinic, he might not have dared to go see his son for the first time. They seemed to have come to a collective agreement not to acknowledge him, and the one person he held out his hand to, Sonia's father, didn't deign to shake it and instead simply gave a curt *thanks*. There was also a brother who must have been about his age and who seemed to be making every effort not to leap up and crack his skull open right then and there. The room was narrow and crowded, and although there were younger girls squealing excitedly, the air was heavy with a sadness that felt terse and disappointed; everyone seemed to be holding back in some way or another, and when he walked in, he felt all eyes turn indiscreetly on him, as though he were wholly responsible for the unhappiness of the situation. Finally, he saw Sonia, lying in bed, the baby on her chest. She didn't look like herself; her features seemed thicker, and she had the same phony regal air—conditioned, almost—as all the people surrounding her. She regarded him solemnly and then smiled, asking everyone to leave them alone. Her request was met with a not insignificant show of displeasure by the majority of the entourage, and then came a truly ludicrous moment when Sonia's brother approached her and, glancing warily at him out of the corner of his eye, asked, "You sure you're going to be OK?" as though really wanting to know, "How can we be sure he's not going to *rape you again?*"

"Have they been horrible to you?" Sonia asked when the two of them were alone.

"Sort of."

"Look. Don't you want to see your son?"

She placed the boy into his arms. It was shocking how hideous he was, and how small. The first thing he noticed was his lightness, an unusual lightness, as though he were nothing but the fruit of a feeling. Then, the fact that he looked wet, and unnervingly guilt-ridden. He didn't look like either him or Sonia. Was it really possible to know a baby? The only thing he knew about him was that he was there, that he was attempting, now that he was awake, to figure out where his little body stopped and started, to train it. He understood—though he wasn't yet at the stage of actually feeling—the emotion, an emotion that formed part of a greater sort of love, a love he'd never experienced until that moment. Sonia was in a better mood now that she was alone with him.

"What are you going to name him?" he asked

"Antón, after his grandfather," she replied.

"Your father?"

Sonia nodded. He took the baby's tiny glove off and examined his hand.

"What's this for?"

"So he doesn't scratch his face with his fingernails. He can't control his little hands yet."

"Listen . . ."

Sonia eyed him with concern; she didn't want any big declarations, and suddenly he, too, felt incapable of making them. He was still holding the baby in his arms, feeling his warmth and strangeness. It was extraordinary, his simple way of just *being*, the whole thing seemed to him like a children's story whose moral was yet to come. He held a finger out, and Antón grabbed it with fingers that looked almost sinister, so tiny were they. He took in Sonia's smell, a sweetish smell of sensitive flesh. She now wore the same sprightly expression she used to, birdlike.

"Don't make that goofy face," she said.

Finally he laughed, for the first time.

"You look goofy," she repeated.

"Oh, do I?"

They were silent for a moment. On the other side of the door, Sonia's family could be heard making a commotion, increasingly restless.

"You should probably go," she said.

For the first year of Antón's life, Sonia continued to live with her parents, which made it impossible to see his

27

son with any regularity. He'd see him occasionally, nearly always when she took him for walks in the Parque del Retiro. They'd meet close to the main entrance, at the Puerta de Alcalá, and from there, walk to the artificial lake in the park. They had less and less in common. Sonia had just finished her degree and begun working as a psychologist, was planning to open her own office once she felt "suitably qualified", and she'd often practice on him, telling him what his *biggest problem* was.

"Your biggest problem is that you don't think life is *real*," she once said—after having told him, in similar circumstances over recent months, that his biggest problem was his fear of commitment, that his biggest problem was his relationship with his mother, and that his biggest problem was that he didn't know the meaning of the word *progress*. That day, however, Sonia's words hurt more than usual, perhaps because they hit closer to the mark than usual. Somehow, she'd gone from happy-go-lucky rebel to slightly arrogant and overconfident twenty-five-year-old. He found her unpleasant in several ways: her way of dressing, for instance, had become that of a small, somewhat cynical, self-possessed middle-aged woman, and her way of speaking, assertive, ever ready to draw definitive conclusions. She'd also taken on the annoying habit of calling him "sweetheart", in a singsong voice, as though speaking to a charming little boy, a tiny troublemaker. They—mainly Sonia—would talk about this and that for the first hour and a half, and in the last fifteen minutes, she'd ask him how he was doing, as though secretly ashamed of having monopolized the conversation but unwilling to admit it.

"But let's not talk about me," she'd say with a serene air and professional smile, the smile he imagined she'd use on future patients.

For him, things had started going worse. Their bassist had left and joined another band, and the addition of a new band member had immediately prompted a downward spiral. He almost never wrote songs anymore and was increasingly frustrated at having to play the same two hits over and over, so much so that he reached a point where he flat out refused to do it. The head of the record company, in a bout of honesty, remarked that perhaps it was time to start considering another form of livelihood and suggested he think about doing promo for other bands. It was a good job, the pay wasn't bad, and he took it because he had no other choice. During that period, until Antón turned two years old, it seemed to him that his only undergirding, the one feeling that remained more or less constant, was the desire to see his son from time to time. It was a desire that took the shape of a disconcerting availability—which Sonia dubbed "periodic guilty conscience"—but that he could only describe as the need to "be present." Antón had gone from hideous baby to very good-looking boy, slightly effeminate, and very quiet, so much so that at first, they took it as the sign of a problem. He turned out to be simply an exceptionally tranquil child.

"Lucky me. Honestly, I am so lucky," Sonia would say with the false conviction of a parent secretly longing for a noisy, rambunctious child.

He'd begun to say a few words, or at least Sonia claimed as much, though each time he saw him, the boy shriveled up so much he resembled a little mask. He toddled unsteadily, always toward Sonia, and seemed to fear even the mere possibility of receiving a kiss from him. Antón was only at ease when Sonia was by his side, and if she moved away even slightly or disappeared momentarily, he'd stare up at him with tiny, terrified eyes. He thought then that the child couldn't have developed everything on his own, that some part of himself must, of necessity, have filtered down to Antón—his fear, maybe—that the boy must have inherited *something of him*. When he was with him, it was hard to think clearly, it was nearly impossible to find the words to describe the sentiment in its entirety. He liked that he was so well dressed, that he was quiet, liked that he was handsome, liked the expression of concentration he wore when examining something—a blade of grass, a new toy—liked the smell he gave off, a smell of young flesh with a slightly syrupy undertone, which could have been an eau de toilette Sonia put on him. But it was as though he couldn't get past any of those sensations, as though he couldn't rise above them or assemble them into any overarching conclusion. He felt a strange desire, a distinct urge for the boy to be happy, but it also felt as though the desire were something greater than himself, as though it were absolutely out of his reach. At times, he'd find himself trying to forge little alliances with the boy, to establish some common language that only the two of them could understand. He would place a toy in his hand and curl up three fingers as he did so, hoping that he, too, would curl his fingers; or he'd imitate his walk, toddling somberly. Right from the start, he'd given up on trying to make him laugh, he wasn't sure why. It wasn't as if the boy laughed much with other people, anyway, and he hated acting like a clown. In fact, he preferred it when the boy was gape-mouthed in awe, or exhausted and asleep in his stroller, or even crying. He sensed that a sort of breach opened up then, that he could reach into his mind in some delicate, mysterious way.

His mother had only seen the child once, when he turned one and a half, and the mere memory of that day would have been enough to justify her resenting Sonia for all eternity. It only even came to pass because he'd finally exhausted every possible excuse and his mother had begun threatening to show up unannounced at Sonia's parents' house and make a scene, shouting that she was the grandmother and nothing was going to keep her from seeing her only grandson, who, as she saw it, had been kidnapped by a band of real estate speculators.

"I don't care how much money they have, I'll kick their door down if I have to."

Her indignation had reached the point that he finally insisted, for the first time ever, that Sonia let him spend an entire day with his mother and Antón.

"I'll go with you," Sonia said.

"You don't understand. I want us to be alone with him. If you're there, my mother will feel uncomfortable, and I want my mother to be relaxed, to enjoy being with her grandson, even if it's only for one day; I can't believe this is even an issue."

In truth, he was afraid his mother would spend the entire day openly insulting Sonia, whom she'd never even laid eyes on. And perhaps he was also afraid to be alone with the boy. Sonia eventually handed Antón over one Sunday morning at eleven—along with a stroller

31

laden with baby food, diapers, lotions, sun hats, and a two-page list of instructions—after having cancelled on him three Sundays running because "it just wasn't a good day for her." Sonia's fear hurt his feelings, it was a fear of leaving Antón alone with him, a fear greater than herself, as though she were knowingly placing her child into the hands of kidnappers or a band of circus gypsies. It seemed to him that Sonia's entire outlook on society could be seen in that fear, a vision that perhaps she couldn't help, one that contained unconcealed scorn for people like him and his mother.

They had decided on a day trip to the town of El Pardo, where they could have lunch outdoors, since it was a beautiful day. He was supposed to meet his mother in an hour. Things got off to a disastrous start. Antón started wailing disconsolately the second Sonia left him in his charge and walked away. Soon afterward, he heard her voice again. In under twenty minutes, she'd already phoned to see how everything was going.

"Fine," he snapped, "if I have any trouble, I'll call you, don't worry."

Still, he had spent twenty minutes pacing up and down the Gran Vía looking for the cafeteria where he'd arranged to meet his mother, pushing a stroller containing a little boy who was wailing so desperately it was impossible to hide. He'd leaned over several times trying to soothe and pet him, telling him it was OK. He got the feeling that every middle-aged woman he passed was staring at him, casting guilt and suspicion. Finally, he took a seat at an outdoor café, the overstocked stroller bursting with bags of additional supplies, positioned Antón so he could keep an eye on him the entire time, and sat quietly. He used a baby wipe to mop up his tears and snot, and the boy seemed to finally calm down, though he kept his gaze on him—cautious, wary. It was hard to believe, but this was the first time the two of them had been alone together. Completely alone. He ordered a beer while he waited for his mother. Those were perhaps the strangest and most insecure moments of the day, the moments he would replay endlessly in his mind, those fifteen minutes they spent outside at the café—Antón solemn and distant and gazing at him the whole time, and he there with his beer, unable to keep from leaning down and giving him a timid stroke, physical contact that Antón didn't seem to encourage, but didn't shrink from, either. Finally, he held out one of the toys that Sonia had packed, a small, red, metal car that Antón proceeded to turn over, insert into his mouth, and bang himself on the knee with. He stared at the boy greedily, taking advantage of the fact that his attention was diverted, still a bit afraid. It seemed then, for the first time, that a sort of transference took place; he didn't know how else to explain it—a boundless well of emotion, and also pain at the fact that intimacy and natural behavior were not possible between them. Until that moment, he'd only ever sensed it in the vaguest of ways, but now it seemed undeniable. He disliked sappiness and melodrama, had no talent for sentimentality, but he had a sudden feeling of general frailty, as though something inside him had shattered and his throat were tightening in genuine distress. He leaned down to give Antón a kiss, which the boy accepted with indifference, faintly inconvenienced, still gazing at his little red car. He felt the urge to speak the word *son*. He sensed that he was attempting to latch on to the emotion behind the word in the same way a lonely soul latches on to the memory of a happy day.

"You look very elegant," he said.

The boy looked up at him, curious.

"That's right, son, I'm talking to you. You look very elegant. Your father's not as elegant as you are."

It was possible that he'd spoken this out loud simply to be able to say those two words. He wasn't sure. And he didn't have much time to think about it, because at that point, his mother appeared.

Recounting everything that had happened during the day for Sonia—in particular recounting what had led to the scrape on Antón's chin—had taken a titanic effort, and Sonia herself had been more dramatic than ever, watching her son return tearful, raising his little arms up to her like a miniature Ulysses after his short yet interminable voyage. Sonia flashed her most hostile face as she turned to him and said, "You'd better have a good explanation for *this*."

There were no great explanations to give aside from the truth. His mother had been dead set on Antón walking by himself, so he'd stood ten feet away. Antón had taken two faltering steps and then fallen flat on his face. He hadn't hurt himself, it was just a little bump. They used the restaurant's first-aid kit to treat him. The bang had been minor, but the scrape looked a little extreme because it was on the upper part of his chin and he'd managed to scratch his lip a little, too.

"Don't worry, this won't be happening again," Sonia replied, furious.

"What's that supposed to mean?"

"Just what it sounds like, that this will never happen *again*. Look at him, he's terrified, I've never seen him like this before."

He really did look terrified, he had to admit Sonia was right this time.

"My mother bought him a couple of toys, I put them in the bag."

Sonia made a face, opening the bag with a total lack of curiosity as to what was inside, and then curtly said goodbye and turned to go. He watched her walk off a few yards, bending constantly over the stroller, and then lost sight of her after she turned at an intersection.

He never told her what had actually happened that day: the boy had been afraid of his grandmother from the start, been afraid of her and rejected her, been afraid of her and perhaps disgusted by her. His mother had pounced on the boy with such ill-concealed desperation that she'd terrified him from the get-go, and Antón didn't take it well. At that point, he realized instantly that not having Sonia there had been a very bad idea, but there was no turning back. All day, his mother behaved like the somewhat unhinged woman that she was, overexcited one moment and deflated the next, first fawning over him and reviewing her entire family tree in search of resemblances (she spent half an hour swearing up and down that the boy was the spitting image of her great uncle Alfredo), and then gazing at him in melancholy silence, registering the fact that she would never be allowed to take part in his life. Her body was tense, trembling with the immense effort it took to not give in to reality. The boy was a walled city, but his mother approached the day as though the next several years of her life were riding entirely on the success or failure of that afternoon. She'd made plans. Eccentric grandmother plans. He knew exactly what she was doing. He pitied her, but his pity was useless, like all pity. She was fifty-six at the time, and her body was rigid, its presence fierce, more fierce than he recalled having seen since his own childhood. It was unpleasant and heart-rending and difficult to see that the years had not mellowed her in the slightest and that her eccentric nature made her persist more anxiously than ever, made her attempt to find some motivation for her actions, made her insist obstinately. It was in the middle of one of these outpourings that she insisted that the boy take his first steps in her presence and Antón fell flat on his face on the second step. Then, after they fixed him up, she withdrew, and despondency got the best of her.

"I can't get excited about a child I'm only going to see once a year," she announced solemnly, "of course he's afraid of me. How could he not be? And that's how it's always going to be. I don't know what I was thinking all this time."

On the way home, in the car, her cruel streak came out.

"I'd rather just pretend he doesn't exist," she declared, but then, as she was saying goodbye to him and Antón, she started to cry and kissed the boy once again and insisted on running into a store full of cheap Chinese imports to buy him a few toys, "so at least he'll have something *from me*."

She bought Antón a plastic tractor and the one and only rubbery figurine that had piqued his interest, a horrid and undoubtedly toxic Martian of some sort that he spent the remainder of the afternoon trying to keep him from sticking in his mouth. He called her that same night, and the following day, and the day after that. His mother didn't answer the phone for a week.

36

He began to focus on his job, on promoting other bands. He began to enjoy life again. His band had split up for good, to no one's great sorrow. The members had all started getting older, settling down, leading *normal* lives, some more so than others. One by one, they'd shacked up or had kids, changed jobs and even changed cities. There was a new generation of musicians who had more energy than they did, and more affectation. It was a generation he understood relatively well, a generation at times more concerned with its image than with its music; they were less free-spirited and more anxious for success, but also had more energy and more drive. They lived under the ominous boot of novelty and thought they had invented almost everything, because they'd listened to almost nothing, but still, their energy did at times lead to moments of splendor. They were self-centered and ignorant, but they made him laugh, and he got along with them. He could hardly believe he'd been at it for four years. Four more years gone by. During the course of that time, he discovered some things about himself that he'd never suspected: he loved his job. He loved the new relationship he had with music, a relationship that was slightly tangential and yet constant, and he'd developed a singular talent for musical arrangement. In truth, he felt incapable of ever composing another song, and yet he was crystal clear about what the songs he heard were *lacking*. He loved coming across a poorly made demo recorded in some rehearsal studio and discovering the seeds of a band therein. He and a partner took some savings and launched a small record company and started producing a few bands. The first year, they managed to cover expenses, and by the second, they had already turned a small profit and positioned themselves as one of the new independent labels. He thrived on being in the eye of that tiny hurricane, on feeling himself surrounded by the energy of the clubs once more, by the drive of the musicians, their tantrums, their drugs, their petty love affairs, their dramas, jealousies, and triumphs.

His relationship with Sonia, too, had changed significantly over those four years. The episode with his mother had been a turning point. They'd kept their distance for a time, during which Sonia built up a perhaps unavoidable resentment toward him. Resentment at feeling trapped by Antón, at not readily finding someone new, which then led to exaggerated man-hating that she took out on him and expressed via clichés unbefitting her psychological insight.

"Men. You're all sons of bitches, every last one of you."

She'd had two frustrated attempts at relationships and now lived alone with Antón in a place that was too big not to feel lacking in inhabitants. She was a good mother, but a tortured mother. Her attitude annoyed him, but he understood it, just as he understood that there was a struggle going on inside her. Sometimes, trying to talk to Sonia was like venturing into a minefield. She'd decided to quit her job in order to devote herself to raising Antón and making financial investments. She financed the opening of a new restaurant and put money in the stock market. It all went fantastically well, and she made even more money than she had projected. She seemed to have inherited her father's shrewd business sense, to have come to terms with that side of herself with cool but efficient detachment. After careful observation, he'd come to the conclusion that the only thing messing Sonia up psychologically was her emotions, that her way of conducting her love life was the only thing that hadn't changed since he'd met her when she was twenty years old, and that as soon as she approached her love life with the same coolhandedness she approached her professional life with, it would all fall into place—she'd meet someone who was also perhaps a bit detached but nevertheless determined to enter into a pact, and they'd shake hands and get hitched.

Antón was now five years old. He saw him whenever he saw Sonia, every three or four months. It pained him to note how draining, how excruciating those encounters were, for all three of them. Antón had grown into a boy of silent, unsettling beauty. He was vaguely effeminate, perhaps as a result of having been raised solely by Sonia. He gave monosyllabic replies. His body had begun to develop and increasingly resembled his own. He took note of this with uneasiness, this resemblance. As if it somehow made him more aware, in turn, of his own body, and as if the boy's preciosity—a preciosity which could only be seen in certain expressions of his and which he found difficult to describe or even recall—dwelled inside him for weeks after he'd seen him. He had the feeling that anything precious was a sign of fragility, like a distinct tic. The grand total of fifteen or so days that they'd spent alone together over the past four years had all been slight variations on the same day. He'd taken him to soccer games several times, to the movies often, and to visit his mother again on occasion. Every time he saw him, it was like he was both a totally different child and the exact same boy. Every time he saw him, he brought a gift that only seemed appropriate for the previous child, the one he'd been the last time he saw him. And because he never knew what to talk about, he asked conventional questions, to which Antón gave mechanical replies, memorized like the eight times table. They both had a bad time of it, yet they both wanted to see each other.

Thinking of Antón had become as natural as breathing. It was always there, clinging to him like the slimy flesh of a clam, like something possessed despite a total lack of effort to possess it. It was a constant feeling, albeit blunted by a huge number of distorting and mitigating circumstances. Often, it made him feel guilty and jinxed, as though wafting up from the whole situation was an unpleasant odor that was impossible to eliminate. It wasn't a matter of not being friendly. They were friendly to each other, but something inside them had stopped getting needlessly excited at little gestures and overtures. At times, he felt almost like he was waiting to see signs of his own childhood surface in Antón so that he could finally place a hand on his shoulder and say, "I know *exactly* what you're talking about."

And yet they hardly touched. A peculiar sense of physical modesty had developed between the two of them. If their hands accidentally came into contact, he sensed that Antón blushed, and one time, when they were at a soccer stadium trying to leave quickly to beat the crowds, Antón ran all the way around the row of bleachers to avoid having to be picked up. It was hard for him to picture his everyday world, his day-to-day life with Sonia, and at school.

Once, Antón broke his arm, and when he went to pick the boy up, he found him with a cast on his arm and one

40

of Sonia's long scarves tied around it like a sling. The cast was covered in drawings and shaky signatures in children's writing. It struck him, looking down at the cast, eyeing it, that this, like some age-old cave painting, was a reflection of Antón's everyday life, of his friends.

"Where did you get all those signatures?"

"The kids in my class."

"They're nice."

"Yeah."

"What are your friends' names? The ones who drew all those pictures."

It was strange, then, to hear the sound of those unknown names—Pablo, Bárbara, Manuel, Javier, Lola, Rita, Diana . . .

Sonia finally met someone. Though *met* might not have been the word. She'd fallen so head over heels that she was virtually unrecognizable. They'd met at a party seven months earlier, at the beginning of winter, and had been practically inseparable ever since. She talked about him in such rapt yet realistic terms that it made him envious. A thirty-four-year-old lawyer, his name was Javier; he was cultured and sociable, happy and reasonably attractive. Once when he went to pick up Antón, he saw him leaving Sonia's building and knew immediately that it was him. It gave him a good feeling, and he examined the man's face carefully, searching for something that might be a sign, as though examining goat entrails, but all he saw was a man of his age, perhaps a little more timid than him, but expressive.

"Can you believe it? Me, falling in love like this, *now*?"

Love—a love that Sonia swore up and down was the only truly genuine thing in her life aside from Antón—had completely transformed her. Softened her and made her generous, or at least that was how it seemed to him, and maybe even made her smarter, as though she'd developed some form of perceptiveness he'd never known her to have. She looked prettier, too. The explosion of human warmth and joy lent a certain roundness to her cheeks, tinged them with a sort of vibrant glow. It was odd—she spoke less, listened more, showed more patience, seemed finally at peace. At first, he was happy for her and congratulated her sincerely. Then her happiness began to unsettle him in a curious way, as though it were reflected onto him like a shadow, diluting some things and underscoring others.

"We're getting married after the summer," she announced one afternoon.

It was ridiculous, but he had to admit to himself that he was suddenly jealous.

"What about Antón?"

"Antón and Javier get along great. The other day, they spent the whole afternoon alone together; they couldn't get along better. When I got home, I found the two of them laughing their heads off."

"Somehow I find that hard to believe," he retorted, attempting to recall the few occasions when he'd ever seen his son *laugh his head off* and the even fewer occasions when he himself had been the cause of such laughter.

"You want me to swear?"

"That won't be necessary."

Sonia fell silent, as if she had put two and two together.

He had no intention of looking at her or of getting upset, but he did and he was. They were at a park close to her place, the weather was nearly perfect. Her eyebrows were raised, her expression attentive.

"Look at me," Sonia said. "*You're* his father. No one is trying to take anyone's place here."

"What place is that?"

It was hard to believe, but this was the first time they'd ever spoken like that.

"Look, I know I haven't always done the right thing. It's not as though you've shown that much interest, either, but I accept the fact that I haven't always done the right thing, haven't given you enough of a chance. I'm prepared to change that if you want."

At first, he said nothing, and then he said OK, but as he did, he noticed something that felt like his pride being turned inside out, like a piece of clothing about to go into the wash. It was a strange and exotic feeling, not entirely pleasant, as though he'd taken a step that would bring to light everything that had been forgiven up until that point but would now be seen as utter ineptitude. Did he really want that, or did he prefer to have Antón as he'd known him up until then?

"OK."

"Javier and I are going away next weekend. I was planning to ask my parents to stay with him. Would you rather have him spend the weekend at your place? You could take him to the amusement park one day. Antón loves the amusement park."

He felt off-guard and didn't want to put on a front with Sonia. He lit a cigarette to buy some time to think.

He knew exactly how it would turn out—a fiasco, the infuriating feeling of being unable to get through to him, unable to touch him. And yet Sonia's unprecedented offer contained the prospect of Antón spending the night at his place, in the small guest room currently filled with musical instruments, and picturing it had a hypnotic effect on him.

"You think he'll be comfortable with it?"

"He will if you're relaxed about it."

"Sometimes I don't know how to act around him."

"He doesn't know how to act around you, either, but that can change if you just relax, if you both just relax."

Sonia did something inexplicable then. She stroked his cheek and gave him a kiss. A simple kiss, on the corner of his mouth, like a moth fluttering gently out of a coat in a closet.

That was a Tuesday, and he spent the next two days in a peculiar state of euphoria. He cleaned the spare room and the rest of his apartment more meticulously than he had for years. He bought several children's DVDs, making his choices under advisement of a salesgirl at a mall, and stacked them next to the television without much conviction. He very nearly called Sonia—would Antón like *The Rescuers Down Under* more or less than the *CantaJuegos Singalong*? Every so often, he stood staring at the bed Antón would sleep in on Saturday night, as though already envisioning him there. He'd arranged with Sonia to pick him up Saturday morning and take him to the amusement park. Despondency set in at lunchtime on Thursday. He saw a long weekend yawning before him—two whole, never-ending days to be spent with an Antón who would be more silent than ever, more awkward than ever, and him wishing like crazy that their mutual torture would come to an end as quickly as possible. The vision had the stark incandescence of events that are all too predictable. Thursday night, he phoned. He had to hear his voice, had to know if he was looking forward to it.

"Did Mamá tell you where we're going on Saturday?"

"Yes."

"And are you looking forward to it?"

"Yeah."

Never in his life, he thought, had he heard a less convincing *yeah*.

"We can do whatever you want, you know, we don't have to go to the amusement park."

"No, I like the amusement park."

"Well, then that's where we'll go, to the amusement park," he replied, but as though wanting to shout at him, to seek a truce, or to ask truthfully, *Can't you see I'm trying?*

Friday was a busy day, as usual. He had two concerts—bands whose records he'd just put out—and he spent all morning on press mailings and all afternoon making sure everything went OK at the sound checks. He generally liked being there for the sound checks, liked the empty auditorium, the musicians on stage adjusting their volumes. There was something he relished about the nakedness of a space that was empty but soon to be full, the rancid smell, the crackling, electric *pop* of speakers being plugged in, as though the whole scene were somehow emblematic, reduced to its essence. That afternoon, though, the very things he usually enjoyed seemed to reawaken—with notable precision—the hopelessness he felt about the approaching weekend. The concerts were both terrible, the first because the band was pissed off and on the verge of splitting up and gave an apathetic performance, the second because they were too high. Halfway through the second concert, he drank more than usual, had a fight with his business partner, and went off to another bar with a few other musicians who were hanging around. Four hours later, he'd had six drinks and was talking to a thirty-year-old girl whose name he'd forgotten despite the fact that she'd already repeated it twice. She had that formaldehyde look of a rock chick whose teen years were long gone— the long mane of curly blond hair; the tight, black pants; a no longer girlish face; and an attractive, naturally dishonest body—and spoke as though she'd known him all her life. He thought he could probably say almost anything to her, proposition her with little to no flourish, and she seemed to want him, too, seemed moderately enthused.

"Sleep with me."

"Are you married?"

"No."

"I was, up until three weeks ago," she replied.

"I'm sorry."

"Nothing to be sorry about."

They shouted over the music in order to be heard, and every time he leaned in toward her, he took in her sweetish scent and looked down her half-open shirt at skin that was a bit rough and led to small, round-looking breasts.

"Come home with me," he said, persevering.

"Don't you even kiss a girl first?" she asked with a smile that seemed a little sad, as though there were a feeling suspended on the tip of her lips, a whole universe that opened and then immediately closed back up, allowing him to glimpse a past far more glorious than this. He kissed her, ardently, tasting the fruitiness of the rum on her tongue and feeling her body press against his, confirming the contours he'd guessed at while staring at her. They had sex as soon as they got back to his place, stripping off clothes in the living room and tripping their way back to the bedroom together. She had a gorgeous body that didn't entirely go with her face, their sex was awkward, and he took too long to come, which produced in him a muted and faintly enraged frustration that the girl must have picked up on, because when they were done, she touched a hand to his cheek and said, smiling, "Hey, relax . . . Are you OK?"

"I have to get up early tomorrow," he said, looking at the clock. It was almost five in the morning.

"What do you have to do?"

"Take my son to the amusement park."

"He lives with his mother?"

"Yes."

"How old is he?"

"Six."

Speaking about Antón to this girl irritated him, despite the fact that all of her questions seemed friendly enough.

"What's his name?"

"Antón."

"And me?"

"You what?"

"What's my name?"

He fell silent for a moment, trying to recall, and she watched him with a smile that might have been flirty or might have been sad, it was impossible to tell.

"My name is Maite," she said, finally.

"Maite, of course."

"Maite, of course," she repeated, smiling.

Walking over to Sonia's place, he felt worse and worse. He'd showered and changed clothes, but it seemed that his entire body was giving off the sickly sweet stink of booze. He'd eaten breakfast in a desperate attempt to feel better as quickly as possible, but it was a miracle the cigarette he'd smoked afterward hadn't made him puke. He was still thinking of Maite's presence, and it seemed as if his hands, his fingertips, were infused with her scent. When they'd said goodbye that morning, they hadn't even exchanged phone numbers. But despite it all, she was affectionate, and so was he, though in a gloomier and less determined way than she.

"I'll see you around," he said finally.

And, smiling, she replied with no resentment, "Don't be ridiculous. You're too good-looking to say something so ridiculous."

Sonia and Javier looked like they'd been up for five hours, and each had a healthy, robust air about them, with a little weekend bag, ready to go. Antón, too, had his own little backpack with a change of clothes for the two days he would be spending with him. During the entire encounter, his overriding preoccupation was that Sonia not notice anything. He was thankful to Javier for being pleasant and not giving him any looks of reproach. His love seemed so undeniable that he felt a certain sense of disgust imagining the conversation they'd have about him once they were alone, the condescending pity with which they'd comment on how bad he looked, the concern Sonia would express. He hardly even glanced at Antón until they were alone together and walking toward the metro to go to the amusement park. It was a beautiful spring day, and specks of pollen fluttered on the street, dancing whimsically like little, round, white insects every time a car went by. He'd fantasized about this, pictured it for the past five days, yet now that it was here, he couldn't begin to describe how hopeless he felt, how little resemblance this scene bore to his fantasy. Antón didn't even seem excited or particularly happy about going to the amusement park, and he himself couldn't think of anywhere he felt less like going. But there was one thing that was the same as in the vision he'd dreamed up in his head, and that was a resolve within himself: he had no intention of faking anything whatsoever. It was as though he'd given himself a slightly absurd ultimatum: the success or failure of their day together would equate to his success or failure with Antón overall.

"How many times have you been to the amusement park?" he asked.

"Five."

"That's a lot of times."

"Rita, this girl in my class, she's been twelve times."

"Maybe Rita's parents don't know what to do with her and that's why they take her to the amusement park, so they can be *free of her.* Did you ever think of that?"

Antón gazed up at him solemnly. He looked like a girl. A solemn, introspective girl.

"No."

"Well, I bet that's what it is, so you can be glad you've only been five times. You can tell that to Rita the next

49

time she gloats about how many times she's been to the amusement park."

He didn't know why he'd spoken to Antón that way; he'd been unable to stop himself. He was annoyed at seeing him sitting there on the metro looking overgroomed and feminine, annoyed that the boy was silent, and he felt an inexplicable angst, like an urge to destroy everything, including his own happiness. It was a ghastly temptation, a feeling that Antón—despite his age and diminutive size—was an enormous, gaping hole into which anything could fit, into which anything could be hurled. He thought his hands were shaking. His hangover came and went in waves. Fear banished love, banished sentimentality even. Antón held his backpack on his knees and played with a little figure of some sort that was hanging from the zipper. He thought that the boy, too, was vacillating, as though he were having racing, contradictory thoughts.

"What's *gloats*?" he finally asked.

"When someone thinks they're better than you, that's gloating."

They made the rest of the trip in near silence, but the closer they got to their destination, the colder he felt, as though something were distancing him from the boy. It was odd, the distance didn't even seem entirely convincing; it was as though he were allowing the feeling to course through his body in order to ask himself afterward if it had been real or not. He didn't know how to stop. They had to stand in line almost twenty minutes in the sun to get the tickets. He was dehydrated and left Antón alone for just a minute while he went and bought a bottle of water, which he guzzled down as Antón gazed on in terror.

"I was dying of thirst."

"Are you sick?" Antón asked.

"No. Do I look sick?"

"Yes."

Despite his coldness, Antón seemed to have worked out a fairly precise plan as to which rides he wanted to go on. They went to the Seven Peaks, the Launcher, the Pirate Ship, and the Magnetic House. He rode with him only on the first one, and he felt so sick afterward that the whole park seemed like a colossal torture chamber. Strident music blared over the loudspeakers, every child seemed virtually deranged with glee. Every child but Antón. When he caught a quick glimpse of him in the little car, hurtling down from the top of the Coaster, he saw that his face bore the same solemn expression as always, not even the vertiginous descent had managed to alter his features, as though everything he experienced was on mute—his heart pounding, his expectant eyes then widening slightly, the sugary stench of cotton candy, the sound of coins falling from pockets as The Launcher turned its riders upside down, imaginary shackles, kids with expressions as sharp as knives. None of it was entirely innocent, most certainly not Antón's face. When he got off one of the rides, he said to him, "You know what? Of all the kids on that ride, you were the only one not laughing."

To which Antón replied with a shrug of the shoulders, staring down at the tips of his shoes.

"It's not the same."

"What's not the same?"

"The amusement park. It's not the same without my friends," he replied. It was as though he'd suddenly become an adult. A small, disillusioned adult. It riled him that he so readily submitted to his own disillusionment, as though that reaction constituted a sure sign of Antón's true nature. The boy had walled himself off to such a degree that not even disillusionment could reach him.

"You have to learn how to have fun by yourself, too. I've never been bored in my whole life."

"I'm not bored, it's just not the same," he replied with unusual resolve.

"So why weren't you laughing, then?"

"Because I didn't feel like it!" he exclaimed suddenly, raising his voice a bit and staring at him intently. His little brow furrowed, and his face looked as though it were about to go clammy, or as though he'd suddenly steeled himself, willing his little self to *be brave*. He'd picked up the backpack with his clothes in it again and begun playing with the little figure on the zipper to avoid looking at him. The boy's mini-rebellion had been brief, but he wanted to string it out, needed to push it, to see it through to the end.

"Couldn't it be that you're always bored? Couldn't it be that you're actually a boring boy?" he asked, crouching down and grabbing hold of his arms in order to force him to look at him. As he crouched, he felt a sudden unsteadiness. It was something akin to compassion, to a voice beseeching him to stop but then egging him on once more. Antón raised his anguished face as though he had been hurt in a place so private that shame had trounced sheepishness and turned to rage. He realized he was hurting him. The boy writhed as though being gripped by many hands, a whole army of shadows, perhaps, like the ones they'd seen in the Tunnel of Terror and that had made the boy lean into him slightly, seek his contact. Now he was trying to avoid it. He managed to struggle free and charge off two steps, but he easily grabbed him again without even having to stand. He tried to look him in the face. He seemed to be on the verge of tears.

"Well you're not happy, either, not *ever!*" he shouted.

How much longer had they stayed there? He couldn't remember. An hour, maybe two. Antón went on a few more rides: the Ferris Wheel, the Cauldron, and the Crazy Worm. Each time the Crazy Worm's top opened and closed, he saw Antón's face, in among those of the other kids. A tiny, empty face, jaw clenched, little hands clutching the bar tightly, a shadow. The whole of Antón was reflected there—he was that shadow that was too wanly incongruous, too intelligent, that shadow that was no longer drawn to him, those eyes that were no longer drawn to him. His hands looked like they were emerging from beneath a blanket. He, meanwhile, hung his head as though condemned. Everything in him had *slackened*, he didn't know how else to explain it, it had all *slackened* like an over-worked muscle, clenched tight and suddenly going flaccid. He'd given up. He saw his life in the coming years with crystal clarity—Sonia marrying Javier, Javier taking on the role that had never been present in Antón's life; it was simply the natural flow of things. His hangover had morphed into a sort of extreme fragility, of unease. The amusement park made everyone seem drunk as they filed from ride to ride, in silence by that point. From time to time, they'd pass groups of shouting boys, girls having tantrums in front of gift shops. Antón walked among the toys with the detachment of a teenager who doesn't want to appear childlike, as though nothing—no toy, no ride—could rouse his interest. Every time he got off of one ride, he named the next one he wanted to go on, less as a show of desire than out of a need to rid himself of the fascination it had at one point held for him. It was as though the two of them, with the painstaking care of the long-suffering, had privately decided to get rid of every object that had once brought them joy, one by one, like a family preparing to burn their possessions so the invading army can't use them.

On the way back to his place, on the metro, Antón seemed to sit as far away from him as possible, hands folded in his lap. Sadness had descended definitively upon them both. They trudged into the apartment. He was so exhausted that he dropped Antón's backpack by the front door and said flatly, "Do you want to watch a movie? I need to sleep."

"OK."

He led him into the living room, took out *The Rescuers Down Under,* and put it on.

"I've seen this one," Antón said.

"I have another one, too."

Antón glanced at it with disinterest.

"That's OK," he said finally, "this one's funny."

He left him there and went into his bedroom. He collapsed onto the unmade bed, a children's song and the movie characters' shrill little voices coming to him from far off. He fell asleep almost at once, as though a shadow had settled over him. He had a horrific dream: he was traveling on a train, a white train, absurdly elegant, inside of which were tables with ashtrays overflowing with cigarette butts. He had the vague sense of not wanting to be there, of not wanting to go to the place the train was taking him, but he couldn't get off. He heard the rattle of machinery, the metallic clank of the tracks; a metallic sound prevailed throughout the entire dream. A woman entered the coach and sat down facing him.

"Don't you recognize me?" she asked.

"No," he answered.

And the woman made a sad face. Suddenly, she was a beautiful woman, fifteen or twenty years older than him. As though his reply had caused her to age in a single second. Next came a man, a middle-aged man.

"Don't you recognize me?"

"No."

"You and I were once good friends."

The old man (suddenly he, too, was old) had a kindhearted look. He would have liked to tell him that he knew who he was.

"Please, don't forget to give everybody my regards," he said before getting up.

"I'll do that," he replied.

The dream went on, repeating the same pattern. A woman entered, and then another man, and another man. They all asked him the same thing. He didn't recognize any of them. They came in through the rear of the coach, sat down facing him, asked if he recognized them, and then left through the front. He felt increasingly distressed, as though the train were hurtling along faster and faster or the metallic squeal of the tracks were becoming shriller, more intolerable, until finally he rose and tried to run out through the back of the train. When he opened the door, he beheld a sinister sight: standing, in a long line, were dozens of people all chatting animatedly, but the instant they saw him, they all fell silent, like actors backstage, caught off-guard. He couldn't explain what made the scene so sinister. He tried to push his way through, but they began groping him in silence with small, sharp hands. He awoke in a state of distress.

For a few minutes, he put all his attention into staring at the alarm clock, attempting to compose himself. In the distance, he could still make out the sound of the movie, and then Antón's voice, at intervals, as though he were talking to himself. Then suddenly he heard another voice, a female voice. And again Antón's voice, and a reply from the female voice. He got up and walked into the living room. It was Maite, she was sitting beside Antón, they were both looking at the television. They turned in unison.

"Hello," Maite said, getting up.

"What are you doing here?"

"I left my cell phone, but I've got it now. You have a very good-looking son."

"Thank you."

"Maite likes this movie, too," Antón declared abruptly.

"Does she?"

"I have a nephew his age, I think I've seen it eighteen times at my sister's place," she replied, and then, turning to Antón, "OK, Antón, give me a kiss, I have to go now."

"Don't go," Antón pleaded.

Maite turned back to him to say goodbye, smiling as though she didn't want to make a big deal of it.

"I'm leaving, thanks for everything, sorry I just barged in like that."

"Don't go, stay awhile," he said.

"Yeah, stay," Antón insisted.

"OK," Maite answered smiling, "I'll stay, by popular demand."

First, voice. Then, silence. Their evening, too, has its own initial awkwardness. Actually, they spend the first half hour watching the rest of the movie, all three sitting on the floor. He sits beside Maite, who's in the middle, leaning slightly toward Antón. Her body seems to emanate a certain warmth, a different warmth than that of the previous night. Because Maite is next to him, she's the only one he can see. She's less attractive but more easygoing than the night before, exhaustion has lent her skin a sort of grainy quality but also made her more radiant, more peremptory somehow. It's as though he never had sex with her. She's wearing a different style of clothes, less provocative and more youthful: jeans and a blue T-shirt, under which he can make out the contours of a plain bra. They make banal comments about the movie, him in particular, since he's hardly paying attention, and Antón's replies come to him from the other side, explanatory and patient. Something seems to have relaxed in the boy's voice, too. It's his normal voice again, a voice that shows little excitement but is calm, familiar.

Then, when the movie ends, the three of them get up, and for half an hour, they're awkward and uncomfortable in their own skin, sitting on the sofa, getting up, going to get a couple Cokes from the refrigerator, Maite asking Antón about his friends, his classes. The boy stands facing the two of them with his jutting lips, his almond-shaped eyes, tired of loving him and tired of not loving him, wrapped up in the presence of Maite, to whom he speaks quickly and constantly, as though needing to make her aware of many things about himself, as though each one of the things he relays holds the magnificent radiance of something pivotal.

Antón says, "Once, I broke my arm, I fell playing football when I went for the ball, and it didn't hurt *at all.*"

And, "Sometimes, when I go to sleep at night, I pretend my bed is a sleigh and it's sliding through the snow."

And, "The thing I like best in the whole world is drawing."

He thinks, while looking at him, about how he didn't always want him, about how there was a point in his life when things were set, and he was happy, and the boy did not exist. It's a strange, persistent thought, like something pushing him toward a stairway, taking him by the hand, and forcing him *up.* Maybe if the evening didn't feel so relaxed, his thoughts would take a different tone—mean-spirited or angry at the world, at the boy, at Sonia—but the light streaming in is beautiful, and as he sits on the sofa, he can feel the contact of Maite's thigh beside him, though he doesn't acknowledge it. His hangover is almost gone, all that's left is exhaustion and softness, like something that spreads over the boy, over the placidness of the sofa, over the objects in the room. Is he the one to blame? Even blame bounces off him like a bogus attempt at blackmail. *Of course* he's the one to blame, but it hardly matters.

"Do you have any games?" Maite asks.

58

"Sure," he replies, "I have Monopoly around here somewhere."

Then, at the table, the streets of Madrid arranged around the board, little streets, bright streets, faded streets: Ronda de Valencia, Cuatro Caminos, Alcalá, Serrano. The boy's hands look a little bigger, he thinks. The boy's eyes look a little bigger, he thinks. He tilts his head to the left every time he throws the dice, a familiar gesture. He remembers that his mother does the same thing, as though this involuntary tilt of the head could somehow tip the die, make it land on six.

"Try to buy up everything you can on the first round, that's the trick," Maite counsels.

Maite is full of tricks.

"And then on the second round, you put a house on everything you bought."

He understands the confusion of properties, of little houses. He's lined them all up in a row, like a miniature housing development. What else could they do but sit there looking happy and charming? The boy seeks out Maite's touch every time he reaches to pick a card from the stack, and then looks at him, or at least he thinks he looks at him.

"Your turn, Papá."

But the mood of the day lingers, too; it doesn't disappear. Or, more than lingering, it's still going, as if it were something in motion. It's like he can simultaneously see the boy's face now and the one in his memory. The motion has changed the boy's face, which displays a constant look of surprise, like a language comprised of events and intentions, all recent yet keeping quietly to themselves. He lands on Gran Vía and has to pay up. He lands on Cuatro

Caminos and has to pay up. The boy collects the banknotes with greedy delight.

"What are you going to do with *all that money?*"

"Ha!" he responds, stunned, cheeks aflame.

Loneliness becomes a muffled buzz. His own loneliness, but also the boy's loneliness. It's as though he's found his way into some place, as though the staircase has taken him somewhere; it's a new room. He's glad Maite is there, glad to have a witness. He's glad to know that the boy's body is growing, glad to be there, to be lonely. He's glad that he is able to get inside the boy's loneliness, as though entering it were a delicate, complicated maneuver, both stopping and gliding at once. And then he focuses on his face as though for the first time, attempting to describe it to himself: his hair is brown, hangs to the bottom of his tiny ears; his eyes are slightly almond-shaped, like his own; his nose, snub, with wide nostrils, like Sonia's; his lips, full and round. He focuses on his clothes, on the curve of his arms pressing earnestly down on the table, on his concentrated expression. He focuses on his loneliness. Six, three, four, Jail, a house, and every time they pass Go, the glimmering, long-awaited twenty-thousand-peseta bill. And then, suddenly, he understands.

GUILE

Mamá had phoned four times that morning to complain about the girl who took care of her, and each call had been a bit more distressed than the one before. The most recent one had caught her on her way into a meeting at the office, and she'd had to hang up with a terse "I'll call you back." She knew not picking up would have been far worse, would have given rise to at least ten suicidal calls in a row and left her unable to concentrate on anything. It was always the same—whenever this sort of thing happened, she ended up with the same vague sense of having done something wrong, as though she'd inadvertently left the pressure cooker on and then gone out of town. She called her back on her way out of the office.

"She's gone," Mamá said.

"Who?"

"Jazmín."

"Why?"

"Because she steals; I fired her."

She could hear a fraught voice in the background, that of Jazmín herself—"I don't steal, Señora."

"She's still there?"

"Yes, she's packing her things, and I'm standing right beside her so she can't take anything," Mamá replied.

"Put her on."

A strange kerfuffle could be heard over the phone, like a bang and then whispering, followed by a distinct "I haven't stolen a single thing."

"I know you haven't, Jazmín, please, don't go."

"Not a single thing," Jazmín repeated in her small, reedy voice, sounding on the verge of tears, "and she wants to report me."

"Nobody's going to report you, Jazmín. My mother is an old woman, please be patient with her."

"Believe me, I am more than patient with her."

"I know, I'm sure you are, please don't go."

Again, an unintelligible whispering and then a long silence, after which came the heart-rending "But ... I want to, I want to leave ... Will you still pay me for the five days I worked this month?"

"Of course I will, don't worry, but please think about staying."

"I'll think about it."

When she got to Mamá's, all that was left of Jazmín was the cloying trail of her perfume in the air, an unmade bed, and several bottles of makeup remover in the bathroom, beside a hand towel bearing the imprint of an eye, like some sort of relic. Mamá was on the living room sofa, watching television from beneath the Scotch plaid blanket she'd given her last Christmas. For months, she'd been feeling cold all the time, or maybe it was the apartment that was cold. It was impossible to know for certain whether the problem was the heating or Mamá being so immobile, whether it was in fact cold or whether it was only natural that anyone who sat as motionless as Mamá did in that place would end up with the same chronic chill. Often, when she walked in, she found she couldn't believe she'd once lived there, been a girl and a teenager there in those rooms, with that furniture. There hadn't actually been any major changes since she left at the age of twenty, yet somehow it seemed to have fallen into decline, it was almost as though everything there were sending some sort of message.

"Did Jazmín leave?"

"I dismissed her," Mamá responded regally.

"You can't keep doing this to me," she said, slipping up. She hadn't meant to add *to me*. *Doing this* was what she'd meant to say. *You can't keep doing this.* Mamá fired back at once.

"To *you*?"

She paced the living room, without taking off her coat, avoiding both the question and the eyes that, she was sure, were looking her up and down. Mamá's eyes were another thing that had changed over the past two years. They were now covered in a very fine, white film, as though someone had taken an eyedropper and administered two tiny drops of milk. Far from giving her a softer look, though, she felt as though the whiteness had actually hardened Mamá's expression further still, made it more distant yet more intense, too—the look of an animal with cataracts. On the bookshelves were photos of her as a girl, of her father (who'd died when she was ten and of whom she retained almost no memories), of her and Pablo's wedding, of Raquel in London, Raquel in Istanbul, Raquel at the Perito Moreno glacier. Smiling images, frozen in time like crags on a cliff.

"Raquel phoned," Mamá sallied forth. "She says *she* wouldn't have anyone who stole from her in her house for one second."

Raquel lived in London now, worked for a communications firm, and had married her second husband—a milky, skittish-looking Englishman by the name of Donovan—three years ago. She could imagine the conversation perfectly. Raquel only put in appearances in Madrid when it was time to play the brilliant prodigal-daughter. She always stayed with Mamá and always turned up laden with gifts for one and all, like an off-kilter, out-of-season Father Christmas. For longer than she could remember, her relationship with her sister had alternated between frustrating, all-pervading silences and fleeting get-togethers full of phony emotion that left her drained because her personality was so ill suited to pretense. Pablo always referred to Raquel like a hurricane. "When is *Raquel* touching down this year?" he'd ask. In her wake, Hurricane Raquel left a trail of unwearable attire for Pablo, indecipherable little statuettes and porcelain figurines— usually black or metallic—for her, and too-small underwear for the kids. And for Mamá, nine times out of ten, what she left her was the absolute certainty that she wasn't getting the love she deserved.

"Mm. I know what Raquel says."

"You don't believe me, you always side with the Romanians," Mamá insisted, sitting up in indignation, "you never believe a single word I say."

The Romanians was her term for all caregivers, Romanian or not, for every woman who had looked after Mamá, lived with her for a brief period of time. As far as actual Romanians, there had only been two, though they must have made quite an impression, because she spoke about them as though they were the epitome of all things evil.

"Get your things, I'm taking you to my place."

Mamá adopted a plaintive, melodramatic tone at times like that.

"How long for, daughter?"

"A day or two, until we find someone else."

"We're not going to find anything in two days."

"We'll see. Get your things. Unless you'd prefer to stay here on your own?"

"Lord, no."

She tried to contain her fury as she watched her trundle off to her room to pack a little bag; she paced up and down Mamá's living room a couple of times, glanced out the window, and finally sat down on the sofa, flushed, with her coat on and an urge to bury her face in her hands and weep tears of rage and despair. Pablo would get angry, Raquel would call eighteen times that night, she would end up feeling anxious in her own home yet again, feeling like she couldn't get enough air, Mamá would dream up urgent needs every other second. Then would come the guilt, the tears, and with them Mamá's insults—or what was worse, her piteous voice calling down the hall like a doleful puppy, asking whether or not she loved her. The whole sequence would be unleashed like an inevitable chain of events, the same as always, and she would once again be trapped.

Every time she brought her mother home with her, she asked herself the same question: *Where did it all begin?* She'd stop at a traffic light, glance at her out of the corner of her eye, light a cigarette, and become distracted, wondering: *Where?* There had to be a place, a moment, a specific day when things had gone awry. A wave of fear rippled over her, like an electric surge, the ludicrous fear of becoming like Mamá, of turning into her. Mamá's emotional world, like so many of her worlds, revolved solely around herself, but in a sort of *limp* manner, she could find no better way to describe it. Yes, *limp* was the word, like some worn-out rubber trinket that keeps flopping over no matter how many times it's righted. But inside that limp rubber object was a hard heart, a heart that was angry at the world, ready to cause harm if necessary, to cheat, to blackmail, to spurn.

"You know, if I didn't exist, you wouldn't exist," she caught her mother telling her eight-year-old son one time.

"Why would you say that to the boy?"

"Because it's true," Mamá shot back. "Or perhaps you think it's not?"

Really, it would have all verged on the comical had it not riled her so much. Sometimes, she actually did manage to laugh at the situation when she talked about it with Pablo, but whereas Pablo's laughter was healthy and heartfelt, hers became more of a sneer when she was alone. That hadn't always been the case, of course. She could recall that growing up, when she was a girl and a teenager, Mamá's personality had been nervous and energetic. It had taken guts and determination to raise two girls on her own, manage the fabric shop on her own, after being widowed so young. She wasn't an ignorant woman. She wasn't an ugly woman. She'd had a couple of serious suitors after Papá died, one lasting several years. For nearly a decade, the shop had had a long and prosperous life, and Mamá had run it with an iron fist. She remembered one time she slapped a shop girl in front of her for having ruined some silk. She remembered the girl's chin had started to tremble in fury and in shame and that Mamá's expression was unsettling, it seemed to exude strength and conviction, and she felt as if it weren't really her mother she was seeing but—superimposed on her for a second—the face of a woman from long ago, the wife of an emperor.

Mamá's decision to sell the shop was one of the most mysterious moments in her life. Around that time, Raquel had just gotten married to her first husband, and she herself had just moved out. Being alone made her feel ashamed, for some reason, just as Raquel's resolve and Mamá's grit made her feel ashamed. She lived in a naïve world in which almost everything made her blush or feel ashamed. She'd leave her classes at the School of Law feeling ugly and very small, kicking up fallen leaves. When she got back to the apartment where she lived with two other students, she'd gaze out the window at Madrid, thinking it looked like an enormous set, a façade full of different-sized doors. She lost her virginity to a handsome boy after a party at her place, since that seemed to be the only way to not have to see him again, as though his being handsome were some sort of guarantee that she wouldn't be able to sustain his interest for long. She'd wanted to lose her virginity. Her innocence bothered her, and she wanted to get it all out, wrench it from inside her. After that episode, she spent four months being ridiculously promiscuous. She punished herself, imposing promiscuity as an attempt to stop being so bashful, but since it didn't come naturally to her, she ended up getting depressed. Raquel moved to Paris and got separated after three months, and then Mamá called up one day and informed her that she'd sold the shop, just like that, like it was nothing, like saying the price of bread had gone up. She felt a sudden panic at that moment, as though the sale of the shop left Mamá, or her, in a troubling, unprotected position.

"But, what are you going to do now?"

"Nothing, for the time being. I'll see."

"Why did you do it?"

"I never liked that shop."

"I thought you did."

"You've always been a little slow," Mamá replied. She neglected to add, she thought then, *Unlike Raquel*.

That was also about the time she first met Pablo, in the university cafeteria. She'd noticed him on several occasions, but always in a distracted sort of way. He was the sort of young man who walked in and automatically pretended to be looking for someone, then quickly gave up on the endeavor and sat down alone. No one to get too worked up about, no one to think too much about, just one of many young men who were a little timid perhaps, a little unsociable, who fit in at university the way a pigeon fits in at the park for a limited period of time, who moved awkwardly as though never completely at ease, who disappeared without a trace. He wore a beige overcoat that went down to his ankles, and a brown cap, like a mix between an anarchist conspirator and a Dostoyevsky character transposed into some British film. Perhaps that was one thing they had in common from the start—they both dressed as though they'd been rummaging through the donated clothes bags at the local parish. From up close, he had a peculiar beauty, or a dormant ferocity, which unsettled her more than it attracted her. She didn't remember when the first time they spoke had been. She did remember, though, that their first dates had been slightly deranged and exhausting, that Pablo had tried to dazzle her by listing out the last hundred pieces of Marxist theory he'd read, and that he'd hardly let her speak. She remembered that they made love after the second night and that she thought she didn't want to see him again, but that they did see each other again—three, four, five more times—and their dates became increasingly relaxed and enjoyable. On their way out of the movie theater, or on their way into a café, it sometimes struck her that they were two outcasts, and he would occasionally grow pensive and make ridiculous assertions, such as *anything would be better than becoming a lawyer—driving a taxi, for example.* One of those nights, just after making love, she lay there gazing at his naked body. Pablo had fallen asleep in the same position he always did, forearm flung over his face like someone just startled by an explosion. She remembered that *that* was when it struck her for the first time. The thought began to form with a texture akin to that of arrogance. She belonged to him. She thought this as if her own body had objectified itself, and that fact brought her a marvelous sense of calm; her body, her desires—everything was an object belonging to Pablo. Love came first as a violent sense of belonging, and then it was as if that sense of belonging had shattered and given her a remarkable gift in return: Pablo's slightly brusque and quirky kindness, an inconceivable yet commonplace transfer of goods. In those days, when she sat down to study, she'd find herself suddenly overcome by her own joy, as though it had pounced and startled her. At times like that, she didn't care about Madrid and its dry riverbed, its winter sun, didn't care about Sunday lunch at Mamá's (*You're not obliged to come if you don't want to, I'm perfectly fine on my own*), about canon law, about the wallpaper in her ridiculous little college bedroom that Mamá had paid for to start with and that she began to pay for soon afterward herself, working part-time as a secretary at a law firm.

Now, driving Mamá back to her place for the *n*th time, it struck her that maybe that's where it had all begun, at some point during those years. Pablo and Mamá had never hit it off, even at the start; Mamá had purposely rebuffed them by fabricating illnesses the first two summers they were married; she had her first son, and then her second, exactly one year later. Idleness had changed Mamá, turned her into another person, a scheming, sedentary conspirator with a few contradictory melodramatic flourishes thrown in for good measure.

Your own mother, and you don't even respect me, she'd say every time she tried to skip Sunday lunch to go to the country with Pablo and the kids. Their phone calls became indistinguishable, facsimiles of one another (*What did you have for lunch?*), osteoarthritis gave her a constant topic of conversation (*Like dogs sinking their teeth into my legs*), and each time she went to pick her up, it seemed like the same old living room was no longer the same old living room, like Mamá's body was no longer her same old body, as though there were something suspended in the smell of the apartment, something stale, and Mamá's body had shriveled inside it like a houseplant exposed to too much sun.

Her real life took place on another plane, one that ran parallel to Mamá's. She discovered that she was a rather eccentric, festive mother. She took joy in seeing that her kids were happy, that they got dirty playing outside; she looked at herself in the mirror and thought that motherhood had given her face an open, natural look. Sex, too, had changed. She needed it with an anxious, ecstatic compulsion; those were the years when they liked to talk dirty in bed.

Yes, she was sure now, it must have been then—when she was too wrapped up in her own happiness to notice anything—that Mamá had started down the slippery slope of self-righteousness and constant criticism, had started with the attention seeking, the lying, the conspiring with Raquel; it must have been then when the house got cold.

A week later, they had interviewed ten new women. The process had a certain complexity to it, so, in the past, Raquel had sometimes flown in for the weekend to lend a hand. The first step involved going to the parish and to two legitimate-seeming NGOs to ask if they knew of any women looking to work as live-ins with an elderly person. She'd leave an abbreviated and slightly mendacious description looking for someone *young, friendly, with experience* to care for an *easygoing, elderly diabetic woman.* She offered lodging, obviously—a *small, charming, light-filled room* (the *charming* part had been Raquel's idea) where no visitors were allowed—a salary of six hundred and fifty euros a month, one day off a week, and the possibility of a contract if she stayed in service more than a year, after an initial three-month trial period. Sometimes, reading

71

over the *more than a year* part, she almost wanted to laugh. For a week, a string of Daysis, Jazmíns, Saras, Déboras, and Nicoletas had been parading through Mamá's living room. She'd give them a tour, and they would meet the Señora, who dressed for the occasion in a suit they would almost undoubtedly never see her wear again. Mamá would buy a little spiral notebook and a pen and jot down her impressions.

> Margarita
> Ugly
> Ecuador?
> Looks like a thief
> 3 kids in . . . Ecuador?
> Talks too much

After a little while, in would come María, or Mónica, and the entire operation would be repeated. She tried to imagine for a minute what it must be like for any of those young women to walk into a cold living room, see an old woman in a suit sitting there with her collection of fans, jotting things down in a notebook while her daughter attempted rather unsuccessfully to come off as pleasant. At times, she felt all she was doing was putting on a performance, setting a trap, like a children's story in which, after entering the house-cum-prison, the unsuspecting innocent would discover to her horror that the walls were no longer made of marzipan, the doors were no longer candy but had turned into solid metal bars. But these women were stronger than that, or at least they seemed to her to be, with their tacky dresses (most likely,

Mamá would never see them wear those again, either), their overpowering perfume, and their reedy voices. What they were doing, in that charade of benevolence and good intentions, was nothing more than sizing up the opponent before combat, something she didn't think a man would understand. Mamá would get up from the sofa to show her her room, or the Daysi of the hour would go to her side and rush to help her up as though anxious to begin working, when in fact what she wanted was to touch her, to find out if she was going to be able to stand it, to take stock of her scent, her texture. Then Daysi would walk down the hall in front of Mamá, and it would be Mamá's turn to take stock of her.

Daysi
35 but looks 45
Do I like Peruvian food, she wants to know (!)
Selfish

Every time a new woman walked into the living room to be interviewed, she worried that her anxiousness to get it over with, and perhaps her feeling of being a fraud, would be detected. Despite being forty-four years old, she'd never learned to lie, and when forced to do so, she felt like the world or the room were closing in around her like a stomach. The truth was that almost all of them seemed fine to her, the sweet, polite ones because they were sweet and polite, the more reserved and organized ones because she thought they'd hold out longer.

Raquel hadn't come to Madrid to lend a hand that time, but she phoned daily. Interminable, late-night phone calls

73

during which she and Mamá ran through each candidate and then Raquel passed judgment, as though her intuition were infallible over a five-thousand-kilometer radius. The two of them belittled all ten women with Raquel having no other information to go on than Mamá's notes, and she ended up having a bitter conversation with her sister in which Raquel repeated ad nauseam that it was Mamá, not her, who would have to live with the woman in question. It was always the same with Raquel—everything seemed more or less under control, until suddenly the conversation veered sharply and became personal.

"You know, this would all be far more straightforward if you were a little more concerned about Mamá."

"That's easy for you to say; you're in London."

"In London or in Kuala Lumpur, it's equal, the blame is yours."

Raquel's conversation was always peppered with incomprehensible phrases that sounded like literal translations from another language. Raquel herself was like a literal translation from another language, but she still felt increasingly pent-up frustration at these continual misunderstandings with her sister. There were times she wanted to put an end to the whole little drama and ask, honestly and genuinely, *Why is it that we're incapable of loving each other?* But rather than a step toward reconciliation, the question itself would have been an open recognition of failure.

Anita turned up the following day, one of three young women sent from the Hispano-Colombian Center for the interview. Actually, all three of them arrived together, and they had to make them wait in the entryway for Mamá to interview them one by one. From the very beginning, her eyes were drawn to her, mesmerized. She couldn't have been even twenty years old. Her shoulders were slightly hunched, and she had a strange adolescent body, small, ratlike eyes, and fidgety hands that spent the whole interview winding themselves around a hairband. Instinctively, she'd saved her for last. When she walked in, she had the lost look of a new girl being left at an orphanage, and then, all at once, she toughened, as though she'd switched on some entirely different person residing within her, the one she needed. With Anita—although she didn't know it at the time, she discovered it later—that's the way things always were; it was as though a new person sprung up from inside her, a different person, and yet the impression she gave was not that of someone who'd suddenly overcome her inherent shyness but that of someone so neutral she could become sixty different people with equal conviction. She asked her where she was from.

"Medellín, Colombia."

She asked her how old she was.

"Nineteen."

She asked her if she had any family.

"Yes, my mother, my boyfriend, Manuel, and my son, Lolito."

Mamá jotted *Has a son* in her notebook, and then vacillated, pen quivering slightly over the paper, not entirely sure whether or not to add an exclamation point, which, in the end, she did.

She asked how old her son was.

"Two."

"Don't you miss him?"

Anita did something indecipherable then, something that made her feel ashamed of her own question. She turned to the window, then to the photos Mamá had displayed on the bookshelves, and then, without skipping a beat, turned back to them with her unreadable brown eyes. And she smiled. A tenuous smile, so unrelated to the question that she seemed not to have heard it, or to have ignored it. She became convinced, then, that there was something far worthier in Anita. It wasn't just that she was a far worthier person—maybe she wasn't—but that something inside Anita was far worthier than Anita herself even, worthier than her nineteen years, than her tiny, mysterious brown eyes, than her black hair that hung down to her shoulders; it was as though each part of her body were independently alive—her fingernails, her hair, her eyes, those eyes that sat watching her, watery and wide open and small. The smile was neither dismissive nor haughty; she would make no attempt to answer an obvious question with an equally obvious response. Anita smiled the way an Egyptian mask smiles out from the display case in a museum—genteel and vacant, as though she served wiser gods than the ones there. She tried to hide her nervousness.

"Did the people at the center tell you what the salary is?"

"Yes."

"Would you like to see your room?"

"Of course."

When Anita got up to leave the living room, she turned to Mamá to see if she'd written anything else in her notebook. She hadn't. The entry was a brief one.

76

Anita
Has a son(!)

And without knowing why, without even so much as consulting with Mamá, when she walked her to the door, she put a hand on her shoulder and said simply, "The job is yours, if you want it. Could you start tomorrow?"

Anita smiled again.

"Of course."

Mamá didn't say a word.

The two times she tried to describe to Pablo what Anita was like, she failed miserably. It wasn't about her personality, which she knew nothing of, or beauty, which Anita didn't possess. The person who'd moved in to Mamá's place as caregiver, rather than winning out over a cohort of candidates, had laid claim to the position as if by right. When she tried to recall her face, she got lost in a strange haze of impressions. And she felt like the girl had fleeting, mysterious bouts of solemnity; she occasionally seemed distracted, or perhaps frightened, but not by anything occurring around her; it was as though she were abruptly overcome by a thought that was just too sad or too somber. And then she'd snap out of it. She was back. Sadness left behind.

Mamá behaved for the first few days with Anita the way she always did when there was a new caregiver, with a wait-and-see attitude, not revealing her hand. Anita did the laundry, was a decent cook, served lunch and dinner, accompanied Mamá on her walks when it wasn't too cold, cleaned enough so that everything looked spotless on the surface, although on close inspection, it was easy to see that she'd put in just enough effort. She had seen her twice when she went to visit, and thought she was almost born to be a maid—housework made her swell, she flitted gracefully from one side of the apartment to the other like a true maid, simply serving and providing; if she undertook a task requiring physical exertion, she panted slightly, but when she got up, she'd look fresh as a newborn cub.

On one of those visits, she conveniently asked her to go have a coffee at the bar next door to Mamá's building, on the pretext of needing to explain a few things. What she really wanted was to be alone with her, to interrogate her. Anita listened to the information about Mamá respectfully but not particularly attentively. Despite being only nineteen, she didn't seem impatient, she showed no signs of her youth aside from those revealed by her body. When she spoke of her family in Colombia, she sat a little stiller. Her father had died ("It was his time to hang up his cleats," she said, and that was the only explanation she gave), her mother looked after Lolito in Medellín (here she took out a photo—the boy had an indescribable look about him, a mix of scared and comical, dressed in a Spiderman suit; he could have been anyone's kid), Manuel had come with her to Madrid and lived in an apartment he shared with roommates.

"He respects me," she said, as though respect were somehow ineffable, a concentrated quality or a complex mechanism whose balance might be thrown off by anything at all, and she stopped with her lips parted, about to say something else that, in the end, simply morphed into a look of wonder and then a tenuous smile.

Sometimes she seemed like a little girl. She looked at her now and was amazed at how erroneous her recollection had been when trying to describe her to Pablo. To Raquel, all she'd said was that she was competent and cheerful, but on considering those words now, she was shocked at having offered something so unfitting, so far from the truth, to describe Anita. That she was nineteen could be seen in her sense of wonder and the clothes she wore, but something made her suspect she'd experienced great violence in her life, perhaps a single episode, that had somehow left her face or her expression looking like someone attempting to remember a tune. It wasn't just her unusual "absences" but something that could be seen in the way she cared for Mamá, in the way she touched her. Despite being nineteen, she seemed to have already fully apprehended something difficult and disturbing—that when an old person decides to destroy themselves and destroy everything around them, the only thing to do is sit back and watch the show. She wasn't cheerful, but was childlike, wasn't happy, but was optimistic, wasn't active, but seemed to contain the concentrated, motionless velocity of a gyroscope. She used a hasty, spiderlike scrawl to copy down the names of Mamá's medications, and when she took blood samples to monitor her glucose levels, she behaved not like someone administering to another human being but like a scientist taking a resin sample from a tree. She read romance novels that seemed totally unsuited to her personality but with a voracity that was entirely in character, and almost every time she came over, she found the two of them in the living room, Mamá watching television and Anita buried in her book.

"Are you happy, Anita?"

"With what?"

"With my mother. Are you settling in OK?"

"Señora is a difficult woman," Anita replied after a silence, and then she regarded her as though their roles had been reversed and she was the one who might or might not be able to bear hearing certain things. She fell silent again.

"What do you mean?"

Anita smiled, seeming disinclined to add anything further to her statement. It occurred to her that maybe she was afraid she'd lose her job if she was honest, and she felt a desperate urge to turn her into a confidant.

"My mother is angry. At life, at the world, who knows. Maybe at me. She wasn't always this way. She was once very strong, though you may find that hard to believe."

"I know."

She'd never spoken that way to any of Mamá's other caregivers. In fact, she'd always prided herself on having a detached, professional attitude, but there was something about Anita that compelled her to do it, perhaps the desire (it was almost absurd to even think it) to protect her from Mamá, perhaps a strange feeling that there was some sort of bond between Anita and herself, it didn't matter what exactly, some kind of compassion.

And then Anita said, "Your mother is ashamed."

The response was so bizarre that she didn't even dare ask of what.

"Ashamed?"

The waiter appeared to clear their cups, and Anita took the opportunity to conclude the conversation with a smile that turned her back into a nineteen-year-old girl. She looked sorry all of a sudden, sorry to be there, to have colluded, maybe. She tucked back a nervous lock of hair that flopped straight back to its initial position. At that moment, her face looked almost flat, full of miniscule, dark moles that she'd never noticed before.

"What makes you say 'ashamed'?"

"I don't know," Anita replied. "I don't know if my mother loves me or not, either."

That year, it seemed like the holiday season dragged on forever, and Anita's words hung in the air for weeks, as though she'd unconsciously cut right to the heart of the matter. Mamá came and spent Christmas week with them. She was more silent than usual, and in a worse mood. Raquel couldn't be in Madrid that year, having gone on vacation to Buenos Aires. But she called every other day to tell them how hot it was, how pretty the Punta del Este beaches were, how sunburned Donovan had gotten, and how tan she herself was looking.

"And the men, Mamá, now these are what I call handsome men, not like the Brits, I tell you."

While Mamá was speaking on the phone, she glanced at her profile, trying to identify the change. Because there had been a change, somewhere. Something had happened to Mamá, and perhaps to her, as well. She tested out the thought—*she's ashamed*. Since the day she'd spoken to Anita, from time to time she tried out those words in regard to Mamá in different situations: sitting beside her with the kids in the living room, at dinner on Christmas Eve, while helping her shower in the morning. She'd grown used to her naked body. She'd seen it for the first time four years ago, when Mamá was admitted to the hospital with something serious. She'd always been modest, and when she saw it that day, she felt a spasm of astonishment, though she tried to behave naturally. Now she was used to it. The two of them locked themselves in the big bathroom every morning and she undressed her, helped her step into the tub, and turned on the shower to wait for the water to get hot. She moved awkwardly, like a sickly, undernourished girl. Sometimes her astonishment diminished, other times it came flooding back. She thought, *she's ashamed.* Perhaps that feeling mattered only to her, but she felt it would never stop roiling inside her, pressing down on her at times and leaving her short of breath. Mamá's skin was unfathomably thin, and covered in little bruises, marks she got knocking into things. Was that what Anita had actually meant? The shame of those marks, of those little bruises? It was curious, she almost had the urge to phone her and ask, or to tell her that now she understood. Marks on her inner thigh, her leg, by her knee, on her arm, under her breasts, suspended like watery inkblots. Maybe they weren't even bruises but weird vagaries of the skin that simply appeared and disappeared, like sparse vegetation. She understood why Anita took her blood samples and checked her glucose levels as though she weren't treating a human being. She, too, when helping Mamá shower, proceeded as though it weren't really Mamá's body she was touching. Was that what the shame was?

When she ventured to tell people about her Christmas, she found it hard, at this point, to explain what happened next. Pablo bought the newspaper that morning, and as he was checking the winning lottery numbers, he turned to her and hooted.

"Your mother won fifty thousand euros," he said.

At first she thought it was a joke, but when she realized it wasn't, she couldn't tell whether the feeling that pierced her heart clear through was one of pleasure or pain.

"What do you mean?"

"Just what I said, she won fifty thousand euros."

Mamá wept all morning long. She seemed afraid they might say something to her, might stare at her too long. She wept for joy, but it was an ugly, anxious joy, her ticket crumpled in one clawlike hand as she sat before the television lest they make another announcement, saying that it was all a lie, perhaps, that in fact there was no prize money. They were broadcasting the celebrations of the grand-prize winners in a village in Soria, at a sad, squalid little lottery office. Someone poured a bottle of *sidra* over an old man's head, and at the entrance to the place, the woman from the lottery office was being tossed over and over again into the air. The kids got more worked up than usual that year, and she felt a certain displeasure at their delight, which manifested as a sort of secret, greedy desire to receive some gift for themselves. Pablo was the only one to behave normally. He went down to buy a bottle of champagne, ate heartily and happily at lunch, and an hour later was taking his siesta as though nothing had happened. It was a lot of money, but at that age, fifty thousand dollars wasn't truly going to alter anyone's life;

it was simultaneously too much and too little to lead to a radical change, and, besides, how could Mamá's life really change as a result of it? Though in fact it already had—as soon as Pablo announced that she'd won fifty thousand euros, something inside her had contracted, as though her jaws had been tied shut. Her face had become void of expression, but not of tension, and she'd remained very still, breathing wearily, noisily. She said she loved her, as though it pained her.

"I love you, daughter."

A fraudulent attempt at reconciliation, like that glass of champagne that hadn't agreed with her at all but she'd insisted on finishing anyway, taking tiny sips as though it were her arthritis medication. Raquel assured them over the phone that they were going to celebrate that night at dinner, that they'd toast her, and she shrieked with joy over and over and made Mamá cry yet again. When she put her to bed that night, she thought she looked like the kids did after an exhausting day filled with too much excitement. She'd aged brutally.

"Tomorrow we'll collect the money, isn't that right, daughter?"

"I'm not sure if we can, tomorrow."

"We can," Mamá answered, "they said so on the television."

It was on opening her own bedroom door and seeing Pablo reading in bed that she felt the urge to sob, but making a scene wasn't in her nature, so she tried to compose herself while she took off her clothes. When she'd laid down beside him, she covered her face with her hands.

"What a day, huh?" he asked smiling.

She tried to smile and then leaned over and kissed him desperately.

"What's the matter?"

"I need you to fuck me," she said.

Pablo laughed, and then, seeing that she looked serious, grew serious himself.

"Hey, what's the matter?"

"It's like everything makes me feel ashamed."

She wasn't sure why, but she had the absurd conviction that Anita was the only person who could help her. She'd been looking forward to the day she'd take Mamá home, pining for it like a date, and when she saw Anita awaiting them in the doorway, she was flooded with a gratifying sense of tranquility, like a schoolgirl who's aced her exams. The week off had done Anita good, and as she watched them approach, she smiled with that unreadable smile of hers. Sometimes it seemed that within Anita lived an anxious person, one possessed of strange appetites, like a tiny predator that pounced and trapped insects.

"You'll have to congratulate my mother, Anita, she won the lottery this year."

"How much?"

"Fifty thousand euros, we collected the prize money three days ago."

"Congratulations, Señora."

Mamá disapproved of her telling everyone about it, but she had sensed from the start that that was exactly what she had to do, that the lottery was like a dangerous room that had to be kept aired out at all costs. The days after they cashed in the ticket had been strange, too. Mamá seemed to have relaxed a bit, but only at the expense of having aged even more, and as for herself . . . she didn't know what was the matter with her. She saw Mamá as a different person, not Mamá, but a more complicated, reserved, mysterious woman, a woman streaked through with miniscule vices and virtues, as though suspended in time on a branch that was about to break but at the same time sprouting new green shoots everywhere. The last few days, she'd had fleeting bouts of absentmindedness and on three occasions had said things that bore no relation to what was going on around her. After collecting her prize money, Mamá turned to her on their way out of the lottery office and, when she asked her if she was happy, replied, "Tell me something interesting I can do."

"With the money?"

"No, me. You never tell me anything, you never tell me what I should do, tell me something interesting I can do, you always just stand there, staring at me . . ."

She'd let fly like that inexplicably, as though something inside her had suddenly come back to life, robust and incongruent. Now, on seeing Anita, she seemed to be calling up that same attitude, acting as though something displeased her.

"Why do people say you're smart and I'm not?"

"What are you talking about, Mamá?"

"I can think the things you think, too . . ."

Anita showed no sign of astonishment, simply helped Mamá inside. She stayed with the two of them for nearly another hour, as though unable to take her leave, helping Anita unpack Mamá's bag and then preparing an early supper. Night fell quickly those days, with almost no transition, and when it did, the apartment got dark in a way that was cold, impersonal, like an empty office building. Before they knew it, they'd spent half an hour like bats, in near total darkness. She sat in the dining room, which was between the living room and Mamá's bedroom, and smoked a cigarette before leaving. She felt she was hoping to be overwhelmed by certain thoughts, but the only thing that came to her was the vague recollection of having lived in that place as though in a state of transition. No, not even as a girl had it felt like home, though she'd never lived anyplace else. She was always thinking things like *The minute I get out of here . . .* Then she thought of Mamá, with no reproach. She'd been a fearsome mother. She'd been intelligent but not levelheaded, told everyone what she thought of them to their faces, been neither sweet nor sensitive, worked hard for as long as was strictly necessary and then closed herself off in a comfortable but solitary life. Perhaps Mamá was solitary by nature. Even something as simple as that seemed difficult to ascertain now. For years, she recalled hoping Mamá would find another partner, but even that memory, as she sat in the dining room in the dark, was just a feeling. Anita walked in suddenly and, seeing her sitting there in the dark, nearly jumped out of her skin. She was carrying clean sheets to put on Mamá's bed and dropped them in shock. Then she picked them up, laughing, a little nervous.

"You scared me," she said.

"Sorry, Anita, I was off in my own world."

"Ah. The things a woman thinks about," Anita replied, as though echoing the thoughts of a man.

She helped her make the bed, and as they put on the sheets, she asked her about her Christmas. Anita told her that she'd spent it with Manolo at his apartment, that Manolo had drunk a lot, that she'd seen Lolito on Skype, and that it made her sad to see him so grown-up and not have him with her. She liked the perfunctory way Anita provided details about her life, that directness, that strict devotion to the facts. Sometimes she thought she recognized in her things from her own adolescence, the ebb and flow of certain sensibilities. It was strange suddenly—she saw Anita making Mamá's bed and remembered herself doing the same thing when she was nineteen. She seemed to feel a certain reproach for Mamá through Anita's adolescent body. She recalled what Mamá used to smell like then, her clothes, her breasts.

"Is it true that your mother won fifty thousand euros in the lottery?"

The question almost made her smile.

"Yes, it's true."

"That's so much money."

"So, what about you?" she asked. "What would you do if you won?"

It was like a children's game—*If I won a million euros . . .*

"I'd go back to Medellín."

When she left that night, she kissed Anita goodbye, too, for the first time. She went over to Mamá, who was still sitting on the sofa reading her novel, and she bent down and gave her a kiss. For a moment, it seemed a farfetched scene—Anita's subdued expression, Mamá's motionlessness, the apartment; it all seemed a prelude to death. And she was abandoning Anita there, abandoning that nineteen-year-old girl. Perhaps that's why she kissed her, because she felt guilty.

"You've got my phone number. Will you call if you need anything?"

And since she was a little embarrassed and had already turned to leave when she asked the question, both Mamá and Anita replied, in unison.

"Yes."

Then comes the first attack, immediately followed by a second. Anita's anguished voice on the phone, the image of her boys playing with plastic parachutes in the living room, and once she's out on the street, the feeling that the sounds of the city—trucks, cars, other people's conversations— are like strange sounds of war. Even the word itself, *attack*, is bellicose. Anita repeated it three times on the phone, as though they were being invaded, pounded by cluster bombs. The conversation with Pablo ("You stay with the kids, I'm going to the hospital, I'll call you later. Call Raquel.") does nothing to reassure her, in fact gives her another strange feeling, that of calculated, military allegiance. Then, outside, she discovers that there exist two worlds: that of those who take cover, and that of those who head out. She's one of those who head out, but as soon as she does, she realizes that, in fact, what she's heading out toward is something unknown. Even the street is filled with an unsettling lack of familiarity. The only thing she can think is thank God this all happened on a Saturday and she was able to head out immediately. Although *immediately* might already be too late. Sitting in the taxi, she tries to conjure up some touching image of Mamá, as if needing to stockpile ammunition. She has no ammunition. She actually considers calling Raquel, but abandons the idea right away. Then, marching into the hospital, she feels indignant; it's as though each question and each movement were taking a lifetime, all the effort of a lifetime to figure out who someone is, an effort that *she never made.* When she first sees her, Mamá is semi-conscious, Anita there beside her. She looks like she's lost twenty pounds and had her skin glossed with yellowish shellac. She feels nothing. What she feels, rather, is the actual absence of any feeling, as though that absence were in turn an active feeling, one allowing her to advance while making everything inside her retreat, a nonsensical tide that recedes when its presence is most needed. Anita approaches and gives her a shaky hug. It is a desperate hug, a hug full of bones, slightly tremulous, like the embrace of a shipwrecked sailor coming across his first human being, doesn't matter who it is. Or perhaps it does. Mamá speaks in non sequiturs, she's sedated.

"I hate all this," she says.

And she believes it, literally, believes her *I hate all this.* But she immediately speaks again.

"Leave her alone . . . and leave me alone, too, while you're at it."

She thanks Anita for everything she's done and reaches out for her mother's hand, claws for it. *Claws* is an especially apt word. Mamá's five cold, motionless fingers, in hers. She makes an absurd declaration: "I'm here."

Mamá's nerves, Mamá's eyes, those eyes like two adjoining mouths. She stays with her for two more hours, Anita by her side, and feels that everything is still changing—her awake and Mamá dozing, as though their two states were as different as two types of meat. The doctor says it's a miracle she's alive, that at her age, this type of attack tends to be fatal. He has a receding hairline, gray hair, and says this practically on his way out, with the professional indifference and lack of imagination typical of so many doctors. It suddenly occurs to her that stupidity might be inevitably inherent to the medical profession—a necessary stupidity, one required for survival—but the elasticity of the doctor's bearing suddenly flusters her far more than the miracle of Mamá being alive. She forgives him dispassionately—*This man has to leave the hospital and still manage to have an appetite, to sleep with his wife, to pay his mortgage, no doubt he earns an obscene salary*—but the sum of those parts means nothing, doesn't explain his attitude.

"I see in her records that your mother had arrhythmia in the past, and a cardiac episode last year."

"You make me sick."

"Excuse me?"

"You heard me."

She can't understand this aggressive behavior of hers. She's never been an aggressive person. There are things she has yet to learn about herself that she's never even suspected. The doctor walks out without a word, and she feels a forlorn elation at having at least put a dent in his perfect white shell. She discovers and forgets Anita's presence intermittently, but quickly realizes that she needs her to be there, beside her. She also feels something dark, something that seems indecent to her: the feeling that her presence belongs to her, that she's paid for it. But the thought immediately makes her feel ashamed.

And her perception of Mamá seems to have become mythologized, albeit unsteady and vacillating—her mind, her will, her almost harmless malevolence, her penchant for fans and fabrics, her defeated pride, her petty life, all those years spent on a sofa watching television, her suitors who weren't really anybody's type, her secrets, her desire not to die, her inability to accept the consequences of anything. She's no different from any other woman, but the obviousness of that fact doesn't blur her image further, instead defines it to the point of being painful. Later, when night falls, she tells Anita she can go. She walks her to the hospital's main exit, and when they step out of the elevator and head for the door, the city's darkness seems strange, and knowing that Anita is there with her produces an unnerving sense of calm, as though her body were radiating something like iridescence. She almost smiles, realizing she hardly even knows her. She reminds herself of this fact so that her feelings won't again run away with her.

"I'll call when we need you, just go home for now, and don't worry—we'll still pay you for these days."

"I don't care about the money," Anita says, and then she does something unexpected—she shakes her hand. A small, rough, cold hand, like that of a young cub whose fur is about to grow in. She is flooded, then, with a terrifying sense of anguish.

"Well, we'll pay you anyway, it's OK."

It's as though Anita doesn't want to leave.

"What am I going to do now?" she asks.

"Go home, talk to your boyfriend, tell him everything. Take a bath. Make love."

Anita smiles at each suggestion, blushes at the last. She lets out a short giggle, as though poking her little snout out of a cave and feeling the warmth of the sun on the tip of her nose.

"OK," she says.

At that moment, she wants to hug her. Then, after she goes back to Mamá, she phones Pablo.

"I need you here, I need you to come right away," she says.

Raquel arrived the following day, preposterously tan, accompanied by an unhappy Donovan who had trouble hiding his irritation at having had his vacation cut short. She rushed straight to the hospital, as though rather than a daughter she were a paramedic upon whose speed the life of the patient depended. She took one look at Mamá and burst into tears. Donovan stood half a step back, and when he greeted Mamá, he did so as though his British stiff upper lip were no match for Mamá's invincible armada. For her, having spent all night and almost all of the next day—until Raquel's arrival—alone at the hospital with Mamá had been almost unbearably odd. She'd stared at her in the semidarkness for hours, unable to sleep, feeling as though she were entering a forest—it looked like a forest—full of shadows but with broad, light-filled expanses, or maybe like spying on a house, peering into the windows of a house where the people were incapable of sitting or standing in anything resembling a natural position. After a few hours, her attention had focused calmly on all of the things around Mamá: the cardiograph, the little IV drip, the metal bars on the bed frame to keep her propped up, the white chairs, and the small sofa by the nightstand (they'd told her it pulled out, but it turned out to be broken). She'd followed the trail of each of those objects the same way the characters in a children's story follow the trail to the mansion of their quest. Mamá's breathing was ragged and labored. Only a few times in the night had she dared to touch her. They'd had two or three very brief conversations about banal things: which flight Raquel was coming in on, whether Anita had left, what time breakfast would be served. At four in the morning, she asked her whether they'd cashed in her winning lottery ticket.

"Yes, we collected the money, don't you remember?"

"Of course I remember."

"Then why are you asking me?"

It wasn't an impatient or exasperated question. It was odd—even impatience had somehow disappeared. Numbness was an objective reality, like the cardiograph or the white nightstand, though it wasn't actually numbness but something even stranger: patience. A courteous, resigned patience, like that of someone waiting for a person who's always late.

"I asked to see if you'd tell me the truth."

"Why would I lie?"

"So you could keep it for yourself."

She felt a flash of anger and then the desire to be cruel. Patience turned into something anxious, as though she were feeling her way along strange tunnels that were sometimes hot and sometimes cold.

"I'm not going to keep it, don't you worry, you can give it to whoever you like, give it to Raquel if you want, or go home and burn it in the gas heater, one bill at a time."

"You don't love me," Mamá said.

Her reply was one that Mamá appeared not to hear, she didn't even know whether or not it was true but it was one that she needed to say out loud.

"I don't know if I love you or not."

And immediately, she had the theatrical urge to bend over her and weep for hours, and to sob, *That's not true, I do love you, I do . . . Do you love me?* She knew it was possible for that scene to unfold, but it seemed too convoluted.

For the rest of the night, she felt as though her reply were hanging in the air, like a jet contrail. All at once, she had a vague recollection: herself at age six, with Mamá, watching her at the mirror getting ready to go out, her on the bed, Mamá facing the armoire's large mirror, brushing her hair vigorously, smacking the brush against her hair. She'd never before noticed how much the just-back-from-Argentina Raquel resembled the Mamá from when she was six. Donovan made the most of his days, sightseeing in Madrid. She and Raquel spent nearly all day together, with Mamá, in the hospital. Mamá's recovery started looking up, and the doctor she'd insulted that first day turned out to get along very well with Raquel, perhaps just to punish her. His rhetoric began to sound optimistic, within the bounds of pessimism. Now, at least his clichés were more positive.

"She's not a young woman," he said, "but who knows? One can never be entirely sure."

From time to time, the two of them went down to the cafeteria, or took a walk in the little park beside the hospital. They talked almost solely about Mamá, about how well or how poorly she was doing. Raquel always spoke in optimistic terms and fantasized about where she'd take her that summer to continue her recovery. She found it impossible to think that Raquel actually believed what she said, and in her sadness and devastation, she attributed that lack of faith to her own selfishness. On one of their walks, Raquel also confessed that she had a lover.

"Lately things haven't been going very well between me and Donovan."

"I'm sorry."

"Don't be," Raquel replied, and added, smiling, "I'm actually happy."

"Really?"

That, too, was strange—Raquel confiding in her. She thought about Anita. Whether Anita would have lovers or not. She felt mentally drained. She'd never thought about having one herself. She recalled that once, on a business trip, she'd kissed a man, even gone home with him, but when he started taking off his clothes, it all seemed so absurd that she could hardly keep from laughing out loud and left immediately. She could understand how people fell in love, but most of the time when people told her stories like that, she felt like she was surrounded by children who needed to be taken by the hand and told flatly, *That doesn't belong to you.*

"Yes, I'm happy. He's Spanish, but he lives in London. He's married, too. It's all so complicated, isn't it?"

And yet Raquel seemed secretly thrilled that everything was so complicated. It was as though her lifestyle, her speech, possessed a degree of wisdom and resolve, and perhaps also frivolity, that she herself lacked. All she could think to say was, "I'm glad."

In fact, she felt afraid. A strange, vague fear that didn't subside even when she was with Pablo, like the fear experienced by someone who knows they're about to be subjected to physical pain but hasn't yet felt it. Pablo had always gotten along so poorly with Mamá that despite his kindness and the fact that he constantly asked how she was feeling, it seemed unnatural to talk about these things with him. Raquel only heard what she wanted to hear; her optimism and near-total ignorance of what Mamá's life was actually like, and maybe even what Mamá herself was actually like, floored her. There was little trust between them, and she'd never been able to speak candidly to her. She was convinced that the moment she tried to tell her about anything that was worrying her, Raquel would respond by clucking her tongue and declaring, "Nonsense."

That's the way it had always been, and nothing, not even Mamá's situation, was going to change that.

Phoning Anita had been less the result of a logical choice than of a lack of better alternatives. She was relieved, in part, that that was the case. She was also relieved, both of the times she saw her over the course of those several days, at the innocence of their conversation. They arranged to meet downtown and took a walk that ended up, both times, with them sitting in a café because it was too cold out. Walking beside her, she felt the presence of her compact, enigmatic body and made very simple statements that Anita replied to like the caregiver that she was, with brief replies dropped like bombshells.

"You know, Anita, my mother is doing very poorly."

"She's an old woman."

She wasn't sure why, but each of Anita's replies made her smile. And Anita didn't seem uneasy about the outlandishness of the situation, in fact seemed to take their conversations and walks as a natural extension of her job, but, as with Mamá, something in her had changed. She seemed more nervous, more cautious, as though attempting to convey something that couldn't be translated from her own Colombian Spanish to her employer's Castilian. From time to time, she told her somewhat more personal things, things about her childhood and adolescence in Medellín, about her mother, or about her city. She described how when she'd told her mother she was pregnant, she'd locked her in her room, taken a leather strap to her, and whipped her bottom raw. She stated this with no passion and no rancor—as though there were no reason make a big fuss about it—but also with an inexplicable weight to her words, the weight of her own indifference, perhaps. Hearing that kind of anecdote left her with a strange feeling, a feeling that there existed a world in which her honest instincts were useless, a world in which her heartfelt indignation was worthless. Then, at the end of their second meeting, she finally said it. She was wearing a cheap, black coat with a hood, and throughout their conversation had been playing with a pink cell phone that she'd no doubt bought with her first paycheck. She looked like a schoolgirl. She stood before her, pulled off her hood, and came out with it.

"I don't want to see Señora die. Do you understand? I don't want Señora to die *in front of me*."

She said it so impetuously that for a moment it seemed her little face was filled with fury. Then she relaxed and took on a startling beauty she hadn't possessed until that moment. As for herself, she thought she might faint; a sudden vertigo and queasiness overcame her. She didn't know if it was due to what Anita had said or the fact that she'd hardly eaten in three days. She thought she sensed, for the first time in her life, the real possibility of Mamá's death. Not the assumption of it, not the conviction that it would happen sooner or later, but the reality of death and all its coarse obscurity. She felt the cold turn to heat, like an abrasion.

"It's not you, I really like you."

And then she made the most unpredictable declaration imaginable.

"I'd like to be like you."

"Like me?"

"Yes," she replied, as though it were somehow shameful.

"Do you want to quit?" she asked, trying to compose herself.

"Yes. I'm sorry."

"They're about to release my mother from the hospital. Could you stay with her for one more week, until I can find someone else?"

Anita took a moment before replying that time.

"I'll do it for you," she said.

Raquel left the day after Mamá was released, with an angry Donovan who had abandoned all attempts to mask his feelings. Pablo took them to the airport. Mamá cried less when saying goodbye but was more helpless than usual, and she stared pointedly at Raquel as though attempting to send her a secret message—*Don't leave me alone with her.* Her face looked wracked with sorrow. All at once, the boys became hyper—this was the first time they'd seen their grandmother in the hospital—and started horsing around by the bed, almost knocking over the IV drip. She jerked them up by their hands, yanked them almost airborne from the room, and gave each of them a smack in the hallway. Pablo saw and was enraged.

"What did you do that for?"

"So they'd keep still."

"Will you just calm down," he seethed, and took the boys with him to the airport.

Later, as she was collecting Mamá's things from the hospital bathroom, she stared at herself in the mirror and thought that her face had a sort of provincial naïveté about it, thought that hitherto unfelt and profoundly simplistic desires could be seen surfacing on her skin—to love, not to die, to possess—alternating with their opposites, as vivid and simplistic as the former—the inability to love, the powerlessness to stop death, not to possess. She folded and packed everything more slowly and carefully than necessary, until Anita arrived to accompany them. Watching her walk in, she thought she looked more like a teenager than ever, kissing Mamá and then her, and helping her to the taxi. She once more had the same gestures, the same darkness she'd noticed the first day she saw her at Mamá's place, gestures suggesting that even her own life was an accident, but an accident worth celebrating, gestures that seemed

100

to have acquired a surprising, robust superiority. She was nobody's maid. It seemed almost impossible to believe that this was the same young girl who just a couple of days earlier had said she didn't want her mother to die in front of her. She now touched Mamá with almost extraordinary candor, with something approaching distinction, and Mamá responded to that gentility like a queen mother about to make her grand entrance before the court.

"I'll call you soon, as soon as I find someone else," she said as she was leaving.

Anita became very serious then.

"I'm sorry about the other day, I said horrible things to you," Anita replied.

"You didn't say anything horrible."

"Yes, I did," she said immediately, and went on with such authority that it seemed impossible to contest. "Then I wished I hadn't. You don't need to find someone else."

It seemed odd how little emotion there was on Anita's face now. It was as though her words reverberated, a slamming door, resounding over those she'd spoken a few nights ago. She sensed an unbreakable pact being formed between them—love, perhaps, but not just any sort of love, a love like soldiers' love.

"Have you really thought this through?"

"Yes."

The two weeks that followed went by surprisingly fast—back to work and Pablo, and the boys. They were swamped with divorce proceedings at the office. Divorces were always filed for after Christmas, it was so predictable that it had become an inside joke at the firm. When things weren't going well before the holidays, her boss would say,

"As we speak, plates are being smashed by those who'll put food on our tables in January."

She began at nine, meeting with the plaintiffs (ninety percent of whom were women), asking them to tell her about their marriages and their reasons for wanting to split up. They sat in a small, pleasant room in the office and she ordered coffee for both of them, closed the door, took out a recorder, and behaved in a way that would have been unrecognizable to those who knew her; she'd lean in toward the woman (she'd been through the questions so many times she hardly needed to glance down at the list) and, with great professionalism, ask the questions in a way that drew out her narrative. At times, she felt each question had the effect of an emetic. The women nearly always cried. Sometimes honest sobs, like coughs, like physical, bodily reactions; the women were so wrought with anxiety or with humiliation that they cried—she didn't know how else to explain it to Pablo when he asked—as though their bodies were ridding themselves of a toxin. Other times, their sobs were theatrical, or almost theatrical. In that little room, it was impossible to tell truth from fiction. They complained of infidelities, selfishness, humiliation, even physical abuse. They all felt they'd been casting pearls before swine. Nearly all of them spoke with disgust—disgust and outrage, disgust and grief. Some, very few, with forsworn resignation, admitting from the start that most likely no one was to blame. She'd always had a hard time feeling sympathy for them. Though she wasn't a cold woman, it seemed that a slightly cynical instinct kicked in during these sessions, or perhaps it was detachment. The natural distrust that one woman always feels for another, for her pain, for her story, and, above all, for her tears.

Two years ago, one woman had truly astonished her. She gave off a different air from the moment she walked in, seemed calmer than the others, sadder, too. Sad in a real and bewildered way, like someone who's suffered through an ordeal that was simply too much for her age or beyond her comprehension. She was very well-spoken, she must have been a very well-educated, upright woman. She looked like she hadn't worked a day in her life, and that gave her an almost otherworldly air. She was the mother of two boys, seventeen and twenty years old. The elder of the two was a heroin addict. If you took all the real estate her family owned and put it together in one spot, it would have filled an entire Madrid city block. As she ran through the requisite questions and recorded the woman's responses, she was taken with the way she replied—straightforward, resolute, without trembling, and yet displaying tremendous emotion behind every move she made, so deliberate, so rhythmic. She must have been a beauty when she was young, a natural beauty, unaware of it. She recalled that by the end of their conversation, she was utterly captivated and couldn't avoid asking where the mistake lay.

"What mistake?"

"Yours," she said, and then added something unusual: "Well, not just yours. Ours, every woman's mistake."

"Well, I don't know where other women go wrong, but I know where I went wrong, though perhaps it isn't actually a mistake, in the end."

"What was it?"

"I think I've lived a *guileless* life. Does that make sense?"

"No."

"I've lived," explained the woman, "resourcefully, perhaps; I'm not a stupid woman. I have money, and that's enabled me to avoid a great number of hardships, and created others that most people don't generally understand. I have a husband and two sons. One of them very fragile. Throughout my life, even at the worst moments, I've always thought that you could get through the hard times as long as you stood your ground, that if you stood your ground, there inevitably came a time when things went back to normal and everybody went back to being good and noble and patient. I've always thought that life required a sort of tenacity, I suppose that's the way I was brought up, and nothing in my experience had refuted that principle, but now I realize that there is one thing I've never had. I've never had guile. The bad times got worse and I showed no guile, and what's more, I discovered that it's not in my nature, and that's why I'm not sure I can hold out much longer. Now does it make sense?"

Her memory of the conversation ended there, with the woman smiling slightly by way of apology, and with the sense that her body had become larger than it in fact was, and more elegant as well. Her mind went back to that conversation several times during the course of those weeks. Mamá had stopped speaking almost entirely. Anita had told her as much on the phone several times, and she'd seen it herself the two or three evenings she'd stopped by the apartment after work. It was strange, the physical effect it had on her. She'd walk in and see her looking the same as ever, lying on the sofa in the living room under the Scotch plaid blanket, ask her how she was, and Anita would be the one to reply.

"Señora has been very relaxed, she's been sitting there quietly all day. She ate a good lunch, green beans and some yogurt."

She got the sense that there was something cold in Mamá's look, an appraisal of sorts, as though her expression were intended to convey the degree of affection she felt. And the way Anita behaved inside the apartment now seemed strange, too. Now that there was almost nothing for her to do, she seemed busier than ever. She avoided being alone with the two of them and bustled constantly from one place to another, cleaning, making dinner, bringing Mamá a glass of milk, then taking it away as soon as it was empty. In her hands, things seemed to acquire a function different from their true purpose. Sometimes, she thought she was running away, that this excess of activity was her way of running away from Mamá and whatever it was she felt for her; other times she thought it was her, rather than Mamá, that she was trying to punish. In fact, it was all crushingly logical—Mamá's condition, Anita's attitude, her own presence in that apartment that had been hers for so many years, a presence reduced now to the role of unwanted guest, a bump on a log.

When she got home, the residue of those evenings with Mamá and Anita lingered until the moment she closed her eyes, even while making love to Pablo, making her feel somehow orphaned, as though she were not in fact Mamá's daughter, not in fact anybody's daughter, and as though the pleasure of making love were somehow divorced from that feeling and yet also a foundation for it. She would feel suddenly distant toward her own children, and that shamed her, as though having smacked them at the hospital were going to scar them for life, scar their consciousness, as if their little eyes, their intelligent eyes, were going to hold on to the event and, when the time came, pay her back, coldness for coldness. Really, she yearned constantly *to be touched* by them, or by Pablo, or by Anita when she was at Mamá's place. It was a nebulous feeling but powerfully heartfelt. *To be touched*—the very desire seemed, by its mere articulation, to contain its own impossibility—*to be touched, to be swept away by something.*

Looking back, there had been nothing special about the last three days of Mamá's life. It was not in her character to search for hidden signs, and she didn't do it then, either, not even despite the fact that Anita called more often than usual and that one time when she went to visit, she came out with her to do the shopping and they talked for some time. When they left the supermarket and she asked her if she wanted to have a drink before going back to Mamá, Anita accepted with relief. She told her that Mamá had been more confused than usual and complained often of having a headache.

"I don't know how to thank you for what you're doing," she said.

"What?"

"This, all of this, having stayed."

"I don't have anyplace else to go, anyway. Manolo left."

"Your boyfriend Manolo?"

"Yes."

"What happened?"

What had happened was simply that Manolo had met another girl and cleared out. And it had been sudden. No, Anita hadn't suspected a thing. No, she wasn't sad. She didn't know what she was, actually, whether she was OK or not. No, she hadn't told her mother in Medellín, she didn't get along with her mother, hadn't she told her that? None of it would have happened if she hadn't been taking care of Señora. Men, you know, they couldn't be left alone for very long, they couldn't help doing these things. Anita spoke with some difficulty but no reproach, seemed insecure but had a strange, all-consuming dignity. Anita was alone in exactly the same way she had previously been coupled, with what seemed like a sudden sort of indigence, as though she'd spent her whole life barefoot and, upon finally reaching that café, had turned around, surprised to see that everyone else was wearing shoes. She'd lived a guileless life. And now here she was taking care of a woman who might die at any moment, but not even that had the power to scare her. She was no longer nineteen but some timeless age. She'd needed each of those events in the same way a person needs small rocks to climb a mountain. And now she was wearing shoes. Was she, was she wearing shoes? It was hard to say. In the days leading up to Mamá's death, she obsessed over that question. She didn't actually think about Mamá herself, but something else, something perhaps harder to resolve: Mamá's loneliness in the company of someone like Anita. She suddenly pitied her, pitied them both.

It happened at two thirty in the morning, on a Tuesday in early February. It was unspeakably cold, and she remembered using exactly the same words with Pablo that Anita had used with her over the phone: "She had another attack; she's dead."

She remembered how austere the cold felt when she got into the taxi, and her sense of stupor, and that she phoned Raquel three times before managing to wake her up. Her own voice sounded metallic, as though they were both suddenly very strong.

"Mamá died. She had another attack."

"Are you with her?"

"No, I'm in a taxi, on the way. The girl called me."

The girl. She remembered that she'd never used that expression to refer to Anita before and that she did it then for the first time more out of shame than aloofness, as though feeling the need to protect a loved one. *The girl.* She remembered that for the first time in her life, she'd felt sorry for Raquel, for some reason. She imagined her lying there sleepily, Donovan by her side—or perhaps her lover by her side, it didn't really matter—getting out of bed heavily, a middle-aged woman who's lost her looks and knows it but still clings to the gestures of beauty, as though she'd momentarily forgotten.

"I'll catch the first plane I can. Don't move her from the house, I don't want to see Mamá at the mortuary, I want to see her at home. Do you hear me?"

"Yes."

She remembered that she'd hardly noticed Anita when she arrived, that it didn't seem strange for her to be out on the street waiting for her. Mamá was in bed, lying on one side but with her body leaning in the opposite direction, like someone who'd turned and reached over

108

early in the morning to hit the alarm clock but fallen back asleep. One of her eyes was open and the other one closed, and she closed the open eye with her thumb, feeling, as she did, a cold, electric distress. The hair on the back of Mamá's neck was sweaty, and it was thicker than she'd thought it was. She remembered having taken note of that—how odd it was that Mamá's hair was *so thick*. Had it always been like that? She remembered, too, that something inside Mamá seemed to still be throbbing, a sort of tenacity on her body's part, and that she saw then that her legs were curled up under the blanket. She smelled a bit like fart, like the faint fart of a child, and her face didn't look contorted, didn't seem to indicate any great suffering in her final moments. She looked, rather, like she'd been smothered, or like something had simply pushed her into bed. She was shocked, holding Mamá's body—suddenly she realized that she was full of bones, that from one day to the next, she'd become noticeably heavier, or harder. She settled her back down onto the bed and left the room. All at once, she was afraid—of the dark, of Mamá's body, of her smell, of the yellowy light of the bedside lamp. She left the room knowing she wouldn't go back in there alone, thinking that she needed Raquel, and as she turned to go, she discovered that Anita had been in the doorway the entire time, watching her. Just as Mamá's face ultimately still looked familiar, Anita's had changed completely. As though she'd had a terrible fright. Her face had withered and hardened, as though everything that constituted Anita had shriveled up inside her body, become miniscule.

"Tell me what happened."

Anita immediately started to cry. She went to her and put a hand on her shoulder, Anita's tiny shoulder, like a little spring, bobbing up and down with her sobs.

"It's OK, it's all right," she said, and thought, *No, nothing is right. But there's nothing left to go wrong.*

Anita clung to her. Her breath smelled of meat, and she felt it on her neck for five interminable minutes. Something had shattered her love for Anita, too, something cold and rational; she felt nothing for her.

"Tell me what happened."

Señora had called out to her in the middle of the night, told her she didn't feel well. She was scared. Señora had asked her to come closer and grabbed her hand. Anita had let go and run away. Then she'd come back, and Señora was dead, she'd stopped breathing. She went downstairs and ran outside, distraught, phoned her—that was it. She spoke through sobs at first but was stoic by the end, nearly recovered, and asked if she could go now.

"Where are you going to go?"

"I don't know, anywhere."

"No, you stay with me."

It wasn't a request, or a plea, but an order: *You stay with me.* Was that what her money got her, then? She sensed that what she felt coursing through her veins at that moment must have been very similar to what a man felt in a brothel. They sat in the kitchen, and Anita made coffee like a maid, moving like a maid, movements that were slightly obtuse and rather dismissive. She found it touching how naturally Anita navigated Mamá's kitchen, the same kitchen in which she herself would have struggled to find a spoon. She wondered what they were going to do with all that stuff. The four hours she spent with Anita in Mamá's house that night were a blur. She remembered that they didn't speak much but also didn't part for even a second, that they were both scared, that she felt unable to contemplate Mamá's death, and that Anita would burst into tears for no apparent reason. She asked her what she was planning to do now, and Anita said she'd try to find another live-in position, most likely. They did practical things: Anita wrote down her address and bank account details so her last month's pay could be deposited, since it had always been Mamá who paid her, up until then, and she'd done it by check. Every little while, she'd remember with a flash that Mamá was dead there in her room and have absurd thoughts—it made no sense for the bedside lamp to still be on, for instance. Anita told her she was going to go pack her suitcase, and she offered to help. She'd never thought about it until then, but Anita had spent those last few months sleeping in *her* room. Actually, all of Mamá's caregivers had, and if she hadn't minded—or even thought about it, really—it was only because not even when she was sleeping there herself had it seemed like her room. Now, suddenly, helping Anita get her things together with Mamá lying dead in the other room, she felt the same way again; she recalled, with almost asphyxiating intensity, having been a miserable teenager between those four walls and having left them with the same sense of relief Anita was displaying at that moment. She was shocked at the sparseness of Anita's suitcase—three T-shirts, two sweaters, four pairs of panties, and several pairs of tights. Six novels, one picture of Lolito dressed as Spiderman, one picture of Manolo, an alarm clock, and a toiletries bag. That was it.

The events of that night faded as dawn approached. Raquel arrived sans Donovan early the next morning, on the first flight from London, and when she walked into Mamá's room, she was at her side. After that, everything flew by at dizzying speed—the mortuary, the burial, a strange sense of permanent submission to all of the realities that death unleashes, the filing of death records, the exhaustion, selecting a coffin, opening Papá's tomb (Raquel did that part with Pablo; she had refused to be present), the day of the funeral, the mass held at the cemetery at Raquel's insistence. At each of those steps, there seemed to be a copious excess of logic, broken only by a few exceptional instances—the moment her boys arrived at the mortuary and hugged her, Pablo's kiss, the touch of Raquel's hand when Mamá's coffin was lowered on an industrial-strength pulley system and it inexplicably screeched, making everyone suddenly flinch and shudder. She couldn't remember when she'd said goodbye to Anita, if indeed she had. She recalled having seen her for the last time at Mamá's place, as they were leaving for the mortuary, and that she'd been so flustered that she didn't think about her again until two weeks after Mamá's death, and then only because she'd forgotten to deposit her last month's pay. They'd made the most of Raquel's last few days in Madrid, closing out Mamá's bank accounts and deciding what they were going to do with the apartment, which in the end they put up for sale. Raquel spent almost a week in Madrid, returned to London for two days to work, and then came back for the weekend. She stayed in a hotel the whole time, and each morning, she went there to pick her up. She'd go up to her room, and Raquel would make her wait on the bed while she finished getting ready. She remembered Raquel's sleep smell emanating from the bed, mingled with the soap smell coming from the shower—the intimate details of her sister, so mysterious yet so everyday. They talked about . . . she wasn't sure what, but they talked a lot over the course of those days, especially Raquel, as though there were something inside her suddenly rousing her spirits. It occurred to her that now, they could be friends. A thought that encased another, perhaps sadder, thought: that it had been Mamá who had kept them from being friends until then. In a way, she seemed younger, or at least younger than the last time she'd seen her, just back from Argentina. She remembered that one afternoon, they'd spent almost an hour debating who was better looking, Robert Redford or Paul Newman.

Her thoughts about Mamá were more haphazard and opaque. They swirled back to her over the course of those weeks amid a whole range of other voices and interpretations, the idea of another way of dying, one less irate than the one she'd had, or more tender. Sometimes, when she spoke to Pablo about her, she was suddenly overcome by the feeling that Mamá had died in excruciating pain. She tried not to talk much, and the only time she got truly morose was when Raquel deposited her share of Mamá's money into her bank account. One morning, she went to get money from the cash machine and asked for a receipt and saw that her balance was twenty-eight thousand euros. Then, almost without thinking, she did something that she never confessed to Pablo: she walked back into the bank and made a wire transfer to Anita's account in the sum of five thousand euros.

For several days, she awaited some sign from Anita, a message, a phone call. One afternoon, she actually found herself on the verge of phoning her. She was at the park with Pablo and the boys and walked off a few feet, took out her cell phone, and dialed most of Anita's number. Then she hung up. That was the last time she really thought about her, about the strange creature she'd been when she was with Mamá, about the reaction she might have had when she discovered the money she'd transferred to her. Giving up that money had been nothing. It seemed the money was simply following its natural course, transferring it didn't even strike her as whimsical. She saw something from her childhood in that act; when Mamá wanted someone to run an errand and she and Raquel were playing, she never asked more than twice. Sometimes, if one of the two girls volunteered, when she got back, Mamá would give her a truly extravagant reward in front of the other—a five-hundred-peseta bill, maybe. Once, to Raquel's everlasting envy, she'd even gone so far as to give her one of her jewels. Mamá, who had never been generous, from time to time made gestures like that, reckless gestures that, more than generosity, conveyed a sort of outright scorn for material goods and a mysterious emulation of the way life distributed its profits, with a thousand-to-one return on the most unexpected of occasions. It tickled her to have made a spontaneous gesture—especially to Anita—that could have been Mamá's, and she felt for a minute that her body had been possessed by one of her gestures, as though she were a cup and Mamá's soul had suddenly overflowed from it, like liquid.

She was never entirely sure whether the encounter had really taken place or not. This was more than two years later. She hadn't thought about Anita in at least a year. Her life had resumed, her mysterious, unmanageable, wan, cavernous, and sometimes breathtaking life, her everyday life. The memory of Mamá had mellowed, and her relationship with Raquel had adopted a routine—a monthly phone call and a Christmas visit. Once, she and Pablo had even made a trip to London and Raquel had spent three days taking them around the city. She and Donovan had divorced, and she had a new Spanish boyfriend three years younger than her who worked in the hotel industry and with whom, she privately confessed, she wanted to have a child. Like the spring in a jack-in-the-box, Mamá's death had triggered in Raquel the desire for a child. She herself found the idea ludicrous and selfish, but also carefree and timeless, like the adolescent urge to get a tattoo. She pictured the child Raquel would have as some small, powerful creature, just as egocentric, waggish, and overwhelming as her sister; she thought the train wreck they were sure to produce would be a sight to see, but that despite Raquel's character, the two of them would most likely be good for each other. Mamá's death had had a surprising effect on Raquel; the legendary status she had conferred upon Mamá was so absurd that she became something akin to the kindly old grandmother out of a bad children's story. She'd clung to that fiction with the tenacity of a survivor, needing constantly to believe— despite a lack of rational support for her belief—that she lived a life very different from the life she in fact lived. Sometimes she would grab hold of her arm and speak of

Mamá in languorous, sentimental tones. She knew, the very first time it happened, that she couldn't go against her narrative, that Raquel needed it to be that way, perhaps needed her complicity, as well, so she simply listened to those anecdotes about events she actually remembered, and remembered quite differently, like someone playing telephone. It wouldn't have done any good to explain that, for her, Mamá had, over the past few years, gradually turned into a person about whom it was increasingly difficult to make any assumptions at all, something like her own body, perhaps—at times intimate and comprehensible, and other times distant and dark and full of warm tunnels.

It was after her return from that trip that she saw her. At first, it was just a strange feeling, and for a few seconds, she didn't even think it was her. She was alone at a mall in an area of town far from home and had just happened to stop in to buy a new ink jet for the printer. She was standing there, lost amid the two hundred possible cartridge options, when she thought she saw a figure moving in a familiar way on the other side of the counters to her left. It took some doing to recognize her. Then suddenly, from one moment to the next, she realized that it was Anita. She hadn't seen her in over two years. In a way, she hadn't changed. She must have been about twenty-two, and she still had that childlike, inscrutable face. She no longer looked like a maid. Nor did she look like a normal girl. Instead, she was more like an amphibian creature, a mix of the girl she had known and another one, a somewhat different one, about whom she knew nothing. She would have been unable to articulate the nervousness she began to feel at that moment. It manifested, at first, as a simple bodily reaction, a warm flush, like that of a teenage girl finding herself alone with a boy, inside a locked room; then the feeling spread, like a sound echoing inside her body, drowning everything out, as though something inside her were howling—she didn't know how else to explain it—as though something were howling and she were tied down on her back. Her first instinct was to walk up and say hello, but as soon as she took her first step, she regretted it. Anita was alone, too, and didn't seem to be looking for anything in particular. She wandered among the computer accessories with the absent look of someone who has no intention of making a purchase, someone killing time, as though secretly daring all of those goods to have the courage to seduce her. None of them did, of course. Anita wandered around in a little spring dress, the sort of thing she'd never seen her wear when she was caring for Mamá, a loud, floral-print dress that brushed the tops of her knees, that hinted at the contours of a body that had promised to fill out and then hadn't. The childlike nature of her anatomy seemed to stem not just from the way she moved but also from something in her very makeup, something internal. She didn't know why, but she found it unpleasant, as unpleasant as the troubling idea that Anita's body was built that way as a defense mechanism and, in essence, made her inexplicably resistant to the one true defeat—time.

Anita made a face and walked off. She began following at a distance. As she did, she felt, strange though it may seem, like she was following a trail Anita herself was leaving behind. She didn't know what she was expecting, she simply felt she should position herself such that Anita be the one to accidentally happen upon her, that she be the one to decide what to say, the one to fumble excuses and feign pleasant surprise. It was as though there were a strange sort of balance in everything that was happening—in Anita's legs walking up the escalator to the women's department, and then again to men's, and from there to juniors. She felt alone, shaken, she wasn't even thinking about Mamá, but about something . . . how could she explain it? Something that had died and was closed off, but was still there, in that tacky little floral-print dress, in the movement of Anita's legs, in the black hair cut differently now and worn in a schoolgirl ponytail.

Finally, Anita approached a salesclerk and asked a question. They spoke for a few seconds, Anita gesticulating, tracing out on her chest what seemed to be the cut of a dress. She was pleased to note that she still recognized her gestures, her way of addressing others that seemed distant yet at the same time somehow intimate, both lacking in passion and totally absorbed. The salesclerk went off, and Anita stood there alone once more. Then she turned abruptly to face her and stared. They were ten yards apart, and she had taken refuge behind a counter, pretend-browsing the T-shirts. She bent down to look at the prices, feeling humiliation course through her body, like a warm bath. She looked up. Anita was still there, staring at her. It was just a few seconds, but it was as if the sounds and echoes of the mall were muffled and the two of them were suddenly submerged, as though underwater. Anita walked up to her. She moved slowly, staring at her the whole time. When she reached her, she got a whiff of that peculiar, distinct smell Anita had, like the smell of almonds.

"Please don't follow me anymore," she said.

There was no apparent excitement in her voice, but no irritation, either.

"I'm sorry."

"There's no reason to be sorry. You were always very good to me."

Anita smiled all of a sudden, an enigmatic smile, like an Egyptian mask. She turned and started back down the escalator, feeling, as she descended, a sort of pent-up, accumulated distress. When she got outside, she felt dizzy but walked faster until she reached a small park, and there she sat down on a bench. There was an intense smell of jasmine, or some other overly sweet and slightly suffocating flower. Then, without knowing why, she clutched her stomach and began to cry harder than she'd ever cried in her life. She felt the sobs leaving her body with abrupt, thundering force, as though they were wracking apart not only her body but her very womanhood, her humanity even, her body a hole from which the sobs gushed the same way a geyser gushes from the earth. She cried for nearly fifteen minutes. Then, spent, she pulled herself together a little, went into a restroom inside a café, washed her face, and smiled at her shiny, puffy reflection, at her red eyes and furrowed chin. When she walked back out onto the street, it was with a feeling of lightness she'd never before experienced, as though she were now free from something—from what, she did not know—finally, marvelously, free.

FIDELITY

While making love for the fourth time in her life, Marina thought for the first time (the other three, she'd set out to simply *feel*, to register information) that real physical pleasure—the flickering that came of that bumbling, fondling game—was nothing like any fictional version she'd ever read in a novel. It was odd, but there was something she'd never seen described, that sort of nervous impatience, of sudden deception—pleasure always arrived unexpectedly, it wasn't (and this had been true the other three times, too, but now *it made sense*) a case of choosing to undertake a progression, or a series of stimuli, but something infinitely more interesting, more prodigious, fragmentary; pleasure would surge and wane and then return once more, impetuous, electric, bursting in like a bank robber, ripping off one mask and donning another. Marina was seventeen years old and the school year had just ended for her. Ramón was eighteen and stressed— that was the last thing he'd said before he started kissing her (and one thing led to the other, as they both knew it would the moment they locked themselves in her father's apartment-cum-library)—because they were going to "fry" him on his college entrance exams. *Fry*, he'd said. And the expression, for some reason, had struck Marina as hilarious, as did his face—pliant, both in anticipation of pleasure and in a sort of veiled shame her father's education produced in him.

"Has your father seriously read all these books?"

"These are just a few of them," she replied. "Every three years or so we clear the place out and send, oh, I don't know, at least a third of them—books that don't make the cut—to vintage booksellers, but it just fills right back up. This is the best of the best. If there's one thing this place has, it's books."

Marina liked using that sort of phrase—*if there's one thing this place has, it's books.* Repeating it to Ramón had added, triumphal pleasures, that of semi-humiliating Ramón (who was, without a doubt, going to get *fried* on his entrance exams), and that of the impact made by the apartment her father had rented right beneath their own because his books, literally, no longer fit where they lived. For as long as Marina could remember, there were nothing but books around her, books, heaped in a twisted, radiant mass, like a menacing creature with a life of its own, one that her mother (who barely read) complained of incessantly and with which her father maintained a relationship both proud and intrepid. There was something restless and feisty about that heap, overflowing, like an alchemist's pantry. But no matter what had made her take Ramón there to make love for the fourth time—before he got *fried* on his entrance exams—Marina felt like the place was protecting

122

her now just as it had protected her on the previous occasions (they had always done it on a bed her father had by a window), in the ceremonious light of day. She'd been a little scared the first time, which was why she decided that, if they did it, it could only be in a place that intimidated Ramón, so she'd have at least the same sway over him as he did over her. She liked Ramón the same way you like a big, white bird, one that's not too bright but is majestic and amusing. She wanted to see him naked. Wanted it with a feverish impatience that came off as a sort of lewd, erratic confusion, stored in a box (was that a good description?) since the first time she met him at a friend's party. She liked that he, too, couldn't help but be scared. *I prefer boys who are scared, a thousand times over*, she'd told a school friend, and felt, on saying it, an odd sort of projection of herself, a sign of superior intelligence, as though she could already see herself at age forty, having had thirty lovers, managing a publishing house in Barcelona, and then adding, *When I was a teenager, I was just terrible*. Still, the first times—especially the very first—were strangely puzzling. Ramón had been so scared her father would walk in at any moment that he couldn't relax at all, just wandered among the bookcases, pulling out books at random, books that he obviously had no interest in, and even stood flicking through the photos in *The Origins of Totalitarianism* by Hannah Arendt with such concentration that it was as though he were poring over instructions on what to do next. She went over to him and talked about the book as though she'd read it, in order to humiliate him a bit more, and let her chest rest against his elbow, causing him to blush immediately. Blushing was like a reflex, something cruel and authoritarian. Ramón's blushing made her blush, too.

"Are you sure your father's not going to come down?"

"I'm sure, he's in Turkey," she said, conjuring up the most unlikely country she could think of (in fact, he was at the paper).

"What's he doing in Turkey?"

"Giving a talk, I think, at a literary critics' conference."

For a second, Ramón was on the verge of confessing that he had no idea there even were literary critics' conferences, but instead he turned to her, pinned her against one of the bookcases, dropped *The Origins of Totalitarianism* clumsily onto the floor, and began kissing her neck. Marina felt each of her nerve endings surge, but just a damp, viscous, semi-erect fraction of them, as though Ramón's body were pressing against her in a slightly masturbatory way. They began to undress each other, in silence. Ramón had brought condoms. Marina knew he always carried them, not because he used them, but because it had become a way of bragging among his friends—carrying them around in your wallet and then, when you went to pull out your money, carelessly flashing them. They were both somewhat vain, and they undressed one another as if they weren't embarrassed at all, but she was reassured to note that Ramón had goose bumps, giving him away just as his blushing had before. She suddenly felt as though she were about to leap from the top of a cliff, as though from that point on, they could never even go back to being human, as though they had no names, had only the immediacy of the whiteness, both shocking and celebratory, of the tan line halfway down Ramón's arm, of her own paleness, sudden and insistent.

"You've done it before, right?" she asked him.

And Ramón gave a rather absurd reply.

"Not completely."

"*Not completely?*"

He looked up as though beseeching her not to demand an explanation of what exactly it meant to do it *incompletely*. He seemed to be suddenly at a loss. She helped him out: "Well, do you want to do it completely with me?"

Where, in what book was that described? Marina wondered that now, the fourth time they were doing it. She wasn't referring to the romantic side of things, but the other one. She'd looked at a few porn sites on the internet—in her room, in the dark, with the sound muted—with the painstaking skepticism of an entomologist, and up until now, she'd assumed that the whole coming business was something more or less impossible to control, and bizarrely repeated (consisting, for some reason, of at least three orgasms in a row), and that when it was over, she would be expected to say something along the lines of "*God, I needed that!*" It seemed, though she chose not to dwell on this detail, that not coming straightaway was some sort of failure; at first, she'd pictured it happening with near-comic speed, now it seemed that there was some *muscular* element to the whole thing, that the whole experience, more than a wave (why was it always described as a wave?), was full of knees, bones, stomachs, ups and downs, throbbing, and secretions, as though the body's very nature, or its structure, had proven itself inept when it came to completing the act competently and a kind of lack of finesse were required simply to advance toward a place that made any sort of sense. More than a ripple, it was contorted, painful chaos, at least the first two times. Then, on the third, they did a better job. Now, on the fourth, two weeks before Ramón was going to get *fried* on his entrance exams, as she felt her own pleasure wend its way through her stomach, and as she turned to him and felt awed by his beauty, it seemed that her pleasure was arcing away in two spirals, one toward embarrassment (at the thought that Ramón might tell the other boys, which was not entirely unlikely) and the other toward a grown-up pride at the studied realization that this was something she was going to be good at, unquestionably good at, that she was going to take pleasure doing it and give pleasure as well. It wasn't an abstract thought, but one emotionally bound and tied to Ramón, to his strange body, his particular body, his skinny legs and slightly sunken chest.

"That was perfect," Ramón said afterward. His face had a sort of athletic beauty, the hair at his temples was matted with sweat as though he'd been playing soccer, or, better yet, swinging on a swing for hours. He seemed a bit solemn suddenly, his declaration rather more well-mannered than truthful. Maybe he felt dirty, or maybe he'd just remembered, with renewed intensity, that they were going to *fry* him on his entrance exams in less than two weeks. Marina didn't know how she felt. Just like after the other times, all that thrusting, that contorting and trembling had left her feeling bashful, as if she wanted to put on her clothes as quickly as possible, or to shield herself from her own nakedness by clinging to Ramón. She jumped up and got dressed as fast as she could. As she was pulling on her pants, she heard him say, "What I really should be doing is studying."

She would have liked to fire off a more hurtful riposte, but all she could think to say was, "Well get to it, then."

Ramón got dressed slowly, pensive.

"Yeah, I will. I'm going to get to it. I'll call you in a couple days, OK?"

"Maybe."

Ramón looked at her aghast. The same look he'd have, no doubt, when he found out they'd *fried* him on his entrance exams. Later, when she went up home (since in order to go home, all she had to do was go up a floor), she climbed the stairs slowly, as though it were impossible to hide the fact that she'd been doing it, and she had mixed feelings. She liked those feelings, even though she didn't, even though they were unpleasant; they struck her as literary and meandering. If she had to describe them, she thought, she'd constantly have to backtrack and say that what she'd just said was true actually wasn't, or to add some new, disconcerting, beautiful yet terrible detail, until she'd woven a kind of perverse tapestry. She could still feel pleasure, a sort of vague tingling, as well as shame at not being a little more feminine. She had the sense that her pleasure was unmistakably seeping through her pores, could be seen on her face and in her look, and that anyone even mildly perceptive would pick up on it immediately. For a second, she was afraid. Her mother opened the door, and didn't notice a thing. Her mother never seemed to notice a thing.

"Where were you?"

"Downstairs, reading."

She attempted—replying as she sped past her mother and went straight to her room—to wear the same expression as Clarice Lispector in her photos, a slightly haughty, distant expression conveying that she knew *something* that no one else knew, and that it was something *dreadful*. Lately, she couldn't stand her mother. Her silent, pharmacist's manner, the way she was just *there*, taking up space, made her sick, as did the fact that she resembled her a little, which is why she'd unconsciously fashioned all of her mannerisms and expressions to be as unlike her as possible. It was an aversion that had evolved naturally and implacably, particularly over the past two years. It hadn't always been that way, but it was now; everything was different now, as though she'd suddenly understood the antipathy she felt toward her mother's indolent life at the pharmacy, which was nothing but a money-making machine, toward her white coat, her slightly phony sympathy, all of that sick people chitchat. She thought she was essentially evil and horrid, evil in a passive way, the evil of those who try to arouse pity.

Her father got home that night more tired than usual, and more contemplative. Marina was just finishing dinner with her mother; they'd hardly spoken during the entire meal. Her mother had said that since school was out now and she had *nothing* to do, she ought to be generous and help raise money for a Doctors Without Borders campaign. What irritated Marina, more than the fact that she'd asked her to volunteer for a campaign (which she'd done hundreds of times), was that *generous* of hers, and the assumption (which, incidentally, was entirely on the mark) that she had *nothing* to do.

"Actually, I was planning to start writing a novel; tomorrow, in fact," she replied, fabricating on the spot with such indisputable conviction that it seemed odd she'd never thought of it before.

"What about?"

"About a lake," she replied with no hesitation, "a lake where time stands still for everyone who goes there. It's going to open with a group of people who all go on a trip and end up there—"

But she had no chance to continue, because her father walked in. He had, as usual, two or three books under one arm, new releases he'd no doubt have to review. Even exhaustion looked good on him, gave him a sort of deliberate, arrogant sheen. He had an unbelievably nice body, which meant that all his female friends fell in love with him and always had. He gave them both a kiss.

"Have you had dinner yet?"

The two of them said yes, in unison, to Marina's embarrassment. They were a strange family. They were excitable, becoming enthusiastic without warning, but also bleak and lonely without warning. They were raucous, but only on the inside, and they didn't know how to handle normality. It was as though they were constantly waiting for something to happen. Something to toss them into the air, something to mistreat them, make them react. Only then did they feel like a family.

"Don't worry about me, I'll throw something together in a bit; I think I'm going to go take a shower."

But when he stopped talking, he just stood there, as though awaiting their approval.

"Right, sure," her mother said, "the heat today was *unbearable.*"

It was like a bad play rehearsal, with all of the actors coming in a few seconds late on their lines, making it all seem unconvincing.

"That looks good," her father said.

"What does?"

"That, what you just had for dinner."

"Oh," her mother replied, "it was nothing, there's still some left in the fridge."

In the end, she did sign up to volunteer. She had nothing else to do, and at least it gave her an excuse to be out most of the day. They gave her a Doctors Without Borders vest and told her to work the blocks around the Plaza Callao in the mornings. She was surprised at how sharp and bright the early-summer atmosphere in Madrid was— suffocatingly hot, electrified, and self-absorbed—and at how much personality there was in the Plaza Callao, a place where she'd always felt there was something *missing*. It was nowhere near where she lived, but was definitely one of her favorite parts of Madrid. The constant sense of there being something missing made her feel frivolous, like the open, contagious, uninhibited laughter of a simpleton. Plus, she got a kick out of seeing people's guilty consciences when she told them that for the price of just one cup of coffee a day, they could support a family of three in Sri Lanka for a month, especially if she was explaining this to someone just coming out of the Corte Inglés with four shopping bags. They'd been given a series of statistics like that to throw in at just the right point in the conversation, and each one had an abracadabra effect. It was hard to see the human spirit as anything but preposterously simplistic after observing some of these stimulus-response displays. And more so if she provided the information while glancing

130

out of the corner of her eye—furtively but repeatedly, leaving no room for doubt—at their shopping bags.

"And listen to this, the plastic from those bags—not even the contents, just the cost of the *plastic itself*—would provide for a month's worth of breakfasts."

Sometimes she risked ludicrous exaggerations. And her idealized Sri Lankan family—that *marvelous*, sketchily outlined family, with an adorable little boy whose face was covered in grime, a tireless father who cut cane all day (did they even *have* sugarcane in Sri Lanka, one woman actually asked her), and a mother who cooked nothing but white rice *every single day*—did the rest; the whole family emerged, as if swimming up through the waters of the collective consciousness, their faces slightly malnourished (not overly so), their eyes pleading unbearably as they then plunged into the Madrileños' hearts, but just for a second, and Marina knew it, just for the second it took the Plaza Callao to restake its objective claim on reality—the late-June heat, the twisting looks of giddy lust as the air vent on the Calle Preciados raised women's skirts, revealing what were almost always cellulite-ridden bottoms, panties that had seen better days, and run-of-the-mill legs that were nonetheless enthusiastically celebrated. Solidarity, for all these people, was luxury and collective shame combined.

But after awhile, she'd get bored and wander into FNAC to look at books and CDs. If she was in the mood and could find the metallic security strip without too much trouble, she'd fantasize about stealing them. Theft (the mere idea of theft, in fact, almost detached from the object that had aroused her greed) exerted the same captivating influence over Marina as sneaking glances at other people's diaries, emails not addressed to her, and letters. That was why she liked writers' collected letters, especially if they leaned toward the intimate or embarrassing. That morning, she'd spent almost fifteen minutes skimming through the love letters of Dylan Thomas, curled up in a corner on the floor, until someone came over and told her she couldn't sit there like that. *"You mustn't look too grown up, because you'd look older than me; and you'll never, I'll never let you, grow wise, and I'll never, you shall never let me, grow wise, and we'll always be young and unwise together,"* Dylan Thomas said to Caitlin Macnamara in one of his love letters. Marina thought some day she'd steal that line from Dylan Thomas and use it on someone.

It happened one of those mornings when she was just about to go home for lunch. Nothing out of the ordinary had occurred all morning—she'd taken down twelve people's personal information, handed out fifty or so pamphlets, and a man of about forty-five had flirted with her a little. She was planning to tell Ramón, to make him jealous—those things made Ramón absolutely furious, set him off instantly, like an allergic reaction. That was when she saw him.

At first it was just a fleeting image. Maybe the way he walked was slightly different, or his attitude, or his arm around the girl's shoulder. Even his *size* seemed different, as though he were bigger or something inside him had swelled, which wasn't the case at home. They passed right by, almost brushing against her, as she was sending Ramón her third text. He had several books under one arm, like at home, and the girl had a cloth bag and a summery, floral-print dress. She was no good at guessing ages. She thought the girl was probably about thirty. She hadn't really been able to see her face. She had a nice body, legs that were maybe a little on the short side but slender and graceful, and unusual hips that moved almost as though she were giving a little skip with each step, and as though that demonstrated some sort of female intelligence on her body's part. Her father's head moved back and forth slightly, first toward the street and then toward her; he seemed to be telling a story. They looked like a normal couple, perhaps a bit lopsided in terms of age, but nothing shocking. Marina felt her blood pound, as though for a second she were on the verge of fainting. The Plaza Callao became hyper-real. The paving stones on the Calle Preciados suddenly became inexplicably dense, as did the buildings, and the heat. The forcefulness of each and every object flickered and permeated the crowd, seeming to leave only the two of them intact, as they glided through it all as though on a moving walkway. The flowers on the girl's dress had a hypnotic effect. The dress was pretty, but only just, verging infinitesimally on being ugly, and her father . . . her father both was and was not himself—or perhaps he was more himself than ever, perhaps his everyday expressions, those he made at home, were nothing more than a self-conscious rehearsal for these ones, the real ones. So *that* was how he really walked, *that* was how he really spoke to people, *that* was his real smile. He had the vim and vigor of a self-assured man, looked more attractive yet more distant. She began to follow them as though in a dream, as though all of the stubborn sounds of the street had been turned off and others had been turned on, new sounds, sounds emitted at a different frequency.

Her Doctors Without Borders vest was like a modern-day brown trench coat and low-brimmed hat. She was actually following them at a very short distance. She could have gotten even closer and they wouldn't have noticed, at least not her father. The two of them burst out laughing in unison once, and then a second time, at which point her father lifted his arm from the girl's shoulders, allowing her to catch a glimpse of her profile for the first time. It struck Marina that, without that dress, in the wintertime, in a long coat, the girl would have been as invisible as she herself was now in her Doctors Without Borders vest. She was the kind of woman who only seemed to exist in springtime, or early summer, the kind who are sallow in wintertime and by the end of summer are so tan that they look cheap. Right now (did she herself know this, she wondered?), she was in all her splendor. Her father walked beside her as though in desperate and continual need of her contact, placing his hand close to her waist without touching her, just to graze her dress, leaning in. He was solicitous and animated, all of his gestures rejuvenated. They stopped at a doorway, in the Plaza de las Descalzas Reales, and her father grabbed her by the waist and kissed her. Heat seemed to bubble up from the ground. Then they spoke for a second, almost in a whisper, she fished in her cloth bag for her keys, unlocked the door, and they went inside together. The enormous door banged shut like a performance coming to a close.

She took hours longer than usual to go home that day, too intent on identifying what she felt to let anyone's presence distract her. In fact, Ramón sent two texts in a row that she didn't even read. She forgot entirely about being hungry. She went back to the Plaza Callao, told the volunteer coordinator she'd be back the next day, handed in her Doctors Without Borders vest, and walked down the Gran Vía with the unsettling feeling that every single person she passed had been touched by a secret. First she replayed the whole scene in her mind. The images had an unshakeable, insistent quality about them, and the fact that they were so simple made them somehow gravid. *Her father was having an* affaire. She repeated *affaire* as though she'd read it in a French novel—*une affaire de coeur.*

Marina had been drunk only a few times in her life, smoked marijuana a couple of times, and snorted cocaine once. Of all those artificial states, the one that most resembled what she felt at that moment was the cold, ramped-up clairvoyance of cocaine. She *held* the images in her hand, toying with them. She didn't feel indignant, didn't feel disgusted, didn't feel worked up, either, or pleased; there was nothing pleasurable and nothing hateful, simply a cold, unsettling distress. It took her nearly half an hour to ascertain that what upset her most about the whole thing was not that her father was being unfaithful to her mother (which struck her as reasonably understandable, after all) but that she *hadn't recognized him at first*; it was the simple fact of having seen, not half an hour ago, several gestures that were totally new to her and yet utterly true-to-life, gestures that she herself could have invented from the cache of already familiar, habitual gestures she'd seen in her father. She felt a tremulous, malignant curiosity about that person.

When she got home, she was surprised to find that she felt nothing for her mother. She was in the living room, hadn't been home long, and was cursing the heat. She'd changed into a comfortable dress and was watching television in the living room, taking little sips of iced tea. She liked history programs, that was almost always what she watched, with great interest but without retaining anything, as though they were just white noise. Iced tea and the ecclesiastical confiscations of Mendizábal. She sat down with her for a second, still anxious, as though the image of what she'd seen a few hours ago might somehow impregnate her mother's tranquility, destroy it, like those geranium moths that laid eggs inside the flowers' stems, allowing their larvae to then devour them from within. The documentary showed priests and nuns being expelled with crestfallen, humiliated faces from convents, as though it were a costume party that had come to an abrupt end. Her mother smelled like pharmacy, an odd, neutral smell, and sat with her arms in her lap, the glass of iced tea cupped between her hands (the same way of holding it when it was hot as when it was cold).

"We can have dinner whenever you want, your father's going to be a little late tonight, he just sent me a text," she said.

"Why do you like these historical documentaries so much?" she asked.

She was not skilled at being skillful. She was nervous. She wanted her mother to watch documentaries forever, to sit there in exactly the same position she was in now. She no longer felt any rancor toward her, just a vague sort of fear, that of something approaching. She looked at her in that silly dress, with her lack of beauty, her boundless knowledge of pharmaceuticals, her new haircut that didn't suit her. Why did she feel guilty?

"I don't know," she smiled, "they *soothe* me. I like seeing images from the past."

Marina was embarrassed by the way that every time she was nice to her mother, she responded immediately with affection. She felt there was something bovine about her, something dim. On vacations, she liked to take long siestas and always awoke with the same scatterbrained expression, as if she had no idea who she was or what she was doing there.

"They said on the news that someone found a fetus in a trash can, wrapped up in newspaper. A *human fetus*," she said, glancing over at her for a second before turning right back to the priests' and nuns' faces. Suddenly, on the screen, there was a nun who'd been made to wear donkey ears, with a strange expression on her face as though she herself were trying not to laugh. "I didn't think that kind of thing still happened."

They ate in silence, gazpacho and charcuterie. Marina thought that if she told her mother then and there that she'd seen her father out with a girl, she probably wouldn't even make a face, might even finish her gazpacho with those slow spoonfuls she took, only half full. All of a sudden, for the first time in her life, her naïveté pained her. Suddenly she registered mortification, as though she'd just remembered something.

"How's your novel going?" she asked. "Have you started yet?"

137

"The requirement for journalism got raised, now it's a 6.5. I'd have to get at least a 7 on the exams to get in . . . Where did you say your father was?"

"At the paper."

"Are you sure?"

"Positive."

Anguish endowed Ramón's face with a strange beauty, a frozen, cosmetic look. In the last three days, they'd made love two times, the fifth and sixth for each of them. That time, Marina had experienced it like a succession of vibrations and pops after which she'd found herself in a dense, lush landscape. Sometimes Ramón got a look on his face while staring at her when she was naked that made things happen inside her, things she couldn't subject to examination, things that simply occurred, perplexingly, for a few moments—a feeling of vulnerability that seemed to form part of courtship and of sex itself.

Now that Ramón was lasting a little longer, she had come for the first time. It was an abrupt experience, something akin to an enormous ball bouncing against her, but also penetrating her, then remaining inside her, a huge ball of air that deflated as it entered, slowly, a delicious, enduring sensation. She suddenly had the urge to cry. To cry and to take Ramón's face, his slightly unusual face, in her hands, to hold it the way you hold something unique, a marble head, and caress it, but knowing all the while that her caresses would never *reach* him. She liked the way Ramón, at those moments, would let her gaze meticulously at his face, in silence—his eyelids, his nose, his eyes, the thin outline of his mouth—a human face allowing itself to be

138

examined up close, open and uncalculating, a face finally free from the posturing that protected it, like a brother's face. The closer she looked, the more Marina felt she was slipping down the steep slope she'd been slipping down for the past week. Then, a simple sentence shattered everything.

"I am royally screwed."

"What are you talking about?"

"The entrance exams, I couldn't get a seven *in my dreams.*"

For a second, she'd been tempted to tell Ramón everything. She wanted to see what effect her words would have on his face, or how she would feel saying them. It seemed incredible that twelve days had gone by already, almost two whole weeks since the first time she'd seen her father with that girl. It seemed incredible that she'd been able to see him and not say anything, not put on a phony expression, and that there was nothing outwardly different about the way he acted or looked, nothing different from the way he was every other day. If she took stock of all the things she'd felt since the first time she saw him, it made it seem as though she'd been almost catatonic for the past two weeks. She'd had the same dream three times: she and her mother were at home, and her father had just left. The phone rang, and her mother answered somewhat theatrically. *He left me,* she said, sobbing, *and this time it's for real.* Then she pretended to swoon, and Marina had to run to her aid. But the dream took a strange turn at the end: when she went to help her mother, as she bent down over her, she suddenly saw that her face bore a more immediate panic, as though the first phony attack had brought on a real one, and suddenly, she was dying in her arms. Marina

139

would wake up drained and distressed, feeling like her head had been inside a plastic bag. Her father's face, in the mornings, bore an expression she associated with the nightmare, which made her want to imitate her mother's theatricality from the dream, start sobbing maybe, or even hit him, suddenly hit him squarely in the face, hard, and then when he grabbed hold of her to deflect the attack, stare into his eyes as furiously and fixedly as she could and say simply, *You ruined my life, Papá.* That, thought Marina, would be a sort of veiled way of letting him know that while he might have ruined her life, he couldn't ruin anything else, that he'd lost all the power and influence he'd always had over her. And *that* was what was really tragic, couldn't he see that?

She'd seen him once more, in the same place. She was in the Plaza Callao enlightening a forty-year-old couple as to how guilty they should feel if they compared their good fortune to that of her (far superior) family of Sri Lankans, when she saw them in the distance and darted behind the couple for refuge. Her father was wearing the same clothes he'd had on that morning, a white shirt and blue jeans, and the girl was wearing a different dress from the first time. They were walking further apart this time and may have been more tense than the first day; from the distance she began following them at, it was impossible to tell for certain whether or not they were speaking. They stopped in the same doorway as the first day and went in without saying a word to each other.

That time, she waited until she saw him come out. She stayed on the corner, squatting in the shade so the heat wouldn't kill her, her back against one of the walls of the

Plaza de las Descalzas Reales, reading—in fits and starts—a
book of Sylvia Plath poems she'd begun with enthusiasm
and now found quite boring:

The tulips are too excitable, it is winter here.
Look how white everything is, how quiet, how snowed-in.

Her father was in the building a little over two hours, and
when he came out, he bore the same determined look,
had the same austere, slightly stiff walk that had surprised
her the first day. Her heart was racing a mile a minute.
She knew what she wanted to do, but didn't know how to
go about it. Her wish was an abstract, slightly asphyxiating
thing. It stopped seeming like a good idea the moment
she stationed herself at the door to wait for someone to
come out. She very nearly gave up several times during
the fifteen minutes she waited. She didn't know what she
was hoping to see. Something stark, something shocking,
something domestic, the landscape after the battle. It was
like she was constantly calibrating her emotions in an
attempt to deduce what she felt for that girl. She wanted to
see the object of desire, wanted to learn her name so she'd
know if it was meant to be spoken in a gruff voice or a
rapt one. She knocked on two doors with no luck, and on
her third try, at apartment 3B, the girl she'd seen with her
father opened the door. She looked like she'd just thrown
on a robe to answer the door and a second earlier had
been naked or in her underwear. She had a disturbingly
naïve face, it was like her mouth was the starting point of
everything on it; she was very pretty, but only in a—how

141

to describe it?—submissive way, as though her beauty were simply the result of some intermittent reflex, something unrelated to herself and that she had no control over. Perhaps she was just ordinary. A pretty, ordinary girl, no doubt not too bright, Marina thought, with a shapely albeit imperfect body. It both distressed and excited her that she was naked beneath that robe, as though she, too, like her father, had the indomitable urge to violate her in some way, defile her, as though something had grazed a miniscule but intimate membrane.

"Are you familiar with Doctors Without Borders?"

She went through most of her initial spiel on autopilot. The girl seemed more concerned that the neighbors might see her dressed like that than about listening to her.

"Would you mind coming in for a second?" she asked, in an accent that suddenly struck her as provincial—Galician, maybe?—but faint, and with such a show of good faith that it was clear she was not from Madrid. "I was just getting dressed when you knocked . . ."

"Sure," she said stepping inside. The girl walked toward what appeared to be the bedroom, assuring her once more that she would only be a second. Marina hardly had time, during that almost literal second, to walk into the living room, a small room with several bookshelves but few books, a sofa, and a coffee table, on which sat two teacups and an ashtray with three cigarette butts. The simple fact that she'd gained entry into her home had all of a sudden disarmed her. Everything felt strangely provisional. It was the home of a loner. Marina had never been in a place like it in all her life. A loner, just passing through. It was as though this person's life lacked the energy required even to scratch the surface of those walls. She returned quickly, in the same dress she'd seen her wearing the first day. Now, seeing her like that, she seemed to have regained her initial mystique, to have grown in some prodigious way within that dress; it was dizzying. She got nervous the moment the girl addressed her.

"I'm sorry, I didn't catch *a word* of what you said."

Her voice began to tremble as she repeated her speech on autopilot once more, asking whether she knew that for the price of just one cup of coffee a day, a family of three in Sri Lanka could eat for a month. In the woman's presence (How old was she? Thirty? Early thirties?), even her unassailable family of Sri Lankans lost their gravitas, became absurd, were too grimy and too nice, there in their traditional costumes, on their sugarcane plantation. She tried to smile and felt her chin begin to wobble. Why did she suddenly feel such anguish? It was as though, with no warning, something had whipped her around inside, something akin to fear.

"Are you OK?"

"No."

They both smiled then, a bit stupidly.

"Would you like a glass of water?"

"Yes, please. I think I'm just light-headed all of a sudden, I've been outside all day."

"Here, have a seat."

She sat before two empty teacups on the table. More than two specific, empty cups, they seemed a naked, abstract thing. One of those cups had been her father's. She repeated that to herself, under her breath, trying to force a reaction, but the thought seemed to add nothing.

She didn't know what she'd been hoping to see before entering that apartment. Things had certainly gone much better than she'd envisioned, not even in her wildest dreams had she thought she might actually make it inside the apartment; at best, she saw herself standing at the door, peering between the girl's shoulder and head, trying to grasp some shred, some sliver of something that would enable her to start conjecturing. Reality proved different. She'd gotten there and not only strolled into the house without the slightest bit of difficulty but was now sitting in the living room, probably on the same sofa they'd made love on, waiting for a glass of water to be brought to her. And yet she didn't know how to process the things around her. It was all so stark and seemingly inoffensive that it disarmed her entirely. How much tedium, how much wisdom, how much life, how much *love* was contained in those empty teacups, those half-filled bookshelves, that nervousness, that dress the girl wore? An unbearable heat was coming in through the open window when she returned with the water. Marina gulped it all down at once, not even stopping for a breath.

"Would you like another one?"

"No, thank you."

She was ashamed that the girl was treating her with such gentility, was being nice to her, was a bit shy. She had waited, standing there in front of her, watching her drink, like a kindly nurse at the bedside of a hospitalized patient. She looked sad.

"Sometimes when I'm walking by," she said, to break the silence, "I see all of you out in the plaza, and I wonder *how can those kids stand out in that sun all day long?*"

"I'm only there in the mornings," she said, and stood—because it was awkward to be seated and speaking to someone who had no apparent intention of sitting themselves—and when she did, the girl quickly placed a hand on her arm. The contact was electric, made her hair stand on end, as though her skin were unexpectedly youthful.

"No, don't get up, it's OK."

"Oh, I'm fine, I'll be going now, thank you, though."

"Are you sure?"

"I'm sure."

"You can stay as long as you want," the girl said, most unpredictably.

"I have to go."

She walked her to the door, and as she did, Marina instantly got a faint whiff of something vaguely sexual, just for a second, a sort of jumble of masculinity, as though taking just one step had somehow moved her into an intimate space, and that had changed the shape of everything, made the walls of the house bow in around her.

"Well, bye."

"Aren't you even going to leave me a pamphlet?"

"Oh, right, of course."

The girl smiled. Did her hands tremble as she reached into her bag to pull it out? She thought they did. She remembered that the girl's dress had fluttered and that after she took the pamphlet, she stood looking at it for a minute. Her expression had an odd quality about it, as though her eyes weren't taking in the meaning of the words written on it but simply gliding over them.

145

"I've always liked Doctors Without Borders, maybe I should make a donation."

"We're there every day, in the Plaza Callao, thanks for the water," she said, taking a step toward the staircase. Her whole body feared that the girl was going to give her a goodbye kiss on each cheek.

"What's your name?"

"Marina."

"I'm Sandra."

She couldn't think of anything to do but repeat her name, before rushing down the stairs three at a time.

"*Sandra*."

It occurred to her afterward, a hundred yards or so from the house, her legs still trembling slightly: Sandra didn't want her to go, she wanted someone to talk to, anyone, about anything. Little by little, she was able to recall certain things that she hadn't been overly aware of while she was there but that had made an impression on her retinas, like the fact that Sandra wasn't wearing a bra under her dress, the silhouette of her possibly too floppy breasts, the smell of her body—an impulsive, sexual smell—her submissiveness, her friendliness. Once outside again, she was back in real time, people once more took on the somewhat languorous, sweaty elegance of a June afternoon. Then she was struck by something she hadn't thought of before: she *already existed* in Sandra's consciousness before stepping into her apartment, her father would have already talked to her about her. How would Sandra have pictured the abstract seventeen-year-old girl that was her? And what about her mother? Something else came to her, too: the image of her father *on top of* Sandra, his face buried in her floppy breasts as she stroked his hair and told him he could stay *as long as he wanted,* that he could do *whatever he wanted* to her. She'd heard that phrase in a little porn clip she'd seen on the internet, home videos—this was in her pre-Ramón phase, when she was still investigating. It was a fleeting image, the man leaned over the woman and penetrated her, and she threw her head back and said, *Do whatever you want to me.* Hearing that, she'd been immediately turned on, just as she was now, envisioning Sandra's mouth pronouncing those words. She was turned on against her will, as though there were something animal, something female contained in them, a disturbing surrender. In some dark way, she herself wanted to be able to say those words, to feel her own body surrender, pliant and available, to the will of another. To feel insignificant. To let herself be controlled by the force of *someone else.* But the scene had been too absurd, too concrete—the coffee table, the empty teacups, each with its little teabag shriveled up inside like a dried fig, the impudence of those near-barren bookshelves, the Madrid heat streaming through the window, Sandra's breasts, floppy and insipid, jiggling a little with each thrust, the conviction that she could hurt her, there, on that very sofa, that more than likely she was longing for that pain, the idea of gripping her face in one hand and squeezing it. What could you do to a person who'd just said *do whatever you want to me*? Do whatever you want to me. Do whatever you want to me. Do *what-ev-er-you-want* to me.

Ramon got *fried* on his entrance exams. They took place over two days, and she went to meet him both days when he finished. He was furious when he came out. He kicked a trashcan over and over, destroying it, and said that the whole thing was *fucking bullshit* and that he *didn't give a fuck.* Just two hours later, his fury had turned into a sort of limp humiliation. He seemed like a little boy, and when he told her that he'd made up his entire response to one of the essay questions, start to finish, he almost started to cry. Marina was mortified thinking he might. He was sitting on one of the parterres in Ciudad Universitaria, smoking a cigarette, and his chin began to quiver. She almost wanted to stand up and slap him and say, *Alright, that's enough!* She couldn't muster any pity for him, especially not as she watched his throat constrict just because he was going to fail his exams. She'd fantasized about making love to him that afternoon, but now, seeing him in that state, she had lost all desire for him. She fidgeted, keeping a certain distance, unable to help herself, staring intently into Ramón's face, which now looked strange and a bit unfamiliar, and his arms, and his pinched mouth. She was experiencing a sort of sangfroid.

"You're so good to me," Ramón said, and she writhed as though he'd just insulted her.

"I am not good."

"I think you are."

To Marina it was like something came noisily crashing down.

"I have to go," she said.

"Where?"

"Home."

148

"You want me to walk you?" Ramón asked, and when she didn't immediately reply, he added, "I'll walk you."

An hour later, they were stripping off their clothes in her father's apartment-cum-library. She'd had a curious feeling when they walked in; she thought of Sandra, then stopped thinking about her and, for some reason, thought of her own mother. It was a strange and ambiguous fact, but for the first time, she could almost see their two faces side by side, and she grasped something so simple it seemed absurd not to have realized it up until that moment—they were quite similar. Not exactly in a physical way, but similar. They were two versions of the same woman, docile and mysterious. A woman that seemed to have been born to say to men *do whatever you want to me.* She pictured her mother saying those words.

Ramón kissed her in such a spineless, feeble way that she was on the verge of telling him to forget it, that it wasn't even worth it, but then in a single second everything changed, as though the fury he'd felt on leaving the exam had been triggered. They were already naked, lying on the little bed her father kept there, Ramón was already *inside* her. Until that moment, she'd remained detached, a witness to the scene, just as an experiment, to see what that was like, with a sort of abstract determination, feeling like this time was, in part, a farewell. Then suddenly something changed. His body began to give off tremendous heat, almost feverish. He stiffened and his mouth twisted involuntarily into a kind of sneer.

"Do you like getting fucked?" he asked.

"*What?*"

She sensed that Ramón's face was burning in shame, and then that he immediately renounced that shame and was using extraordinary force with her, as though fearing she might escape, which, in turn, immediately led her to try. There was a struggle of sorts, she couldn't remember it very well. She remembered feeling all of Ramón's weight on her in a second, feeling the almost hermetic way he wrapped his arms around her, so that she couldn't use hers. She remembered that, as he did, Ramón accidentally banged his head on one of the shelves and that she couldn't help but let out a giggle that seemed to provoke a furious reaction in him, like a little boy who's been humiliated too many times in one day and suddenly explodes with rage and starts shouting and destroying everything in sight.

"Just shut up," she thought he said.

"What did you say?"

Ramón looked up.

"I said *just shut up*." But when he repeated it, Marina thought he looked horrified at himself, looked beseeching and utterly wretched, as though he were already pleading forgiveness with his eyes. Then he buried his face in her shoulder so as not to have to look at her. She lay motionless. For nearly a minute, she didn't move a muscle, simply allowed herself to feel all of Ramón's weight on top of her. *Bear*, that was a primordial and particularly apt word: *to bear it*. She didn't feel unhappy, didn't even feel like she was *there*, it was like insomnia, like when you've been awake too long and suddenly the world around you takes on an elastic and yet overly irritating quality at the same time; she thought she stiffened and that her whole being began to exude immense displeasure. Ramón kept moving inside her with the tenacity of a little boy who sets out to break a toy and, discovering that it's harder than he thought, loses the euphoria that drove him to do it in the first place but continues banging it on the floor. There was even a fleeting moment when he raised his head and she could see his profile, and it was like all of his features had been erased in a single stroke, the essence of what he was and the misery of the day he'd just had, it was like faces at a track meet, contorted in pain yet immersed in the unreal world of adrenalin and effort. He came abruptly, thrust her a little further up against the wall at the head of the bed, and stopped moving. He was drenched in sweat. They were both drenched.

"Get up, you're crushing me," she said.

Ramón reacted with immediate submission, but very slowly, and wordlessly. He sat on the bed, unmoving, still wearing the condom, catching his breath. It was impossible to know what was going on inside him, and regardless, Marina didn't care. Everything that had just happened comprised a *truth*, just as Sandra comprised a truth, and her mother and her father. She was miles away. She didn't care about his humiliation, didn't care about his unhappiness, wanted nothing to do with his life. Nor did she want to hurt him; she simply wanted him to go.

"Get dressed, I have to go home."

Ramón turned to her as though in an attempt to say something, to offer an excuse. He opened his eyes wide, regaining use of his conscience, and slid his arm closer until it touched hers. She dressed quickly, and Ramón didn't watch her as she did. He, in turn, dressed slowly. Before opening the door, he turned to her and asked, "Can you forgive me?"

151

"Can I *forgive you?*" she retorted. Ramón didn't exist. Maybe she could say something like this: *You don't exist; how can I forgive someone who doesn't exist?* And yet there he was, his skin the same as the other times, his hair curling slightly and still plastered to his temples with sweat, his burly shoulders, his ineptitude.

"Yes. Can you forgive me?"

She couldn't remember exactly how she replied on that occasion. She remembered that Ramón left and that she went upstairs to the house. She remembered that she came in and kissed her mother mechanically and that she locked herself in the bathroom, slowly took off her clothes, and turned on the shower.

A week passed, strange, dangling, indifferent. She didn't know if she was happy or unhappy, didn't miss Ramón, hardly read. In the mornings, she went to the Plaza Callao to volunteer and in the afternoons, to a friend's pool. The two of them would lie there sunbathing, not talking much, seeing and being seen. The poolside crew, languid and dreamlike, had a hazy, chlorine-flavored soul.

Ramón was sending three or four texts a day, sometimes sweet (*I miss you*), sometimes self-indulgent (*You know I'd never hurt you*), sometimes guilt-ridden (*I can't stop thinking about it*), sometimes informative (*I've already started studying for the September exam, I think I can pass this time*). It was like following the course of his lifeblood, like putting your finger on someone's jugular and feeling their continuous, involuntary pulse. She didn't reply to any of them, and yet she needed them, like notches marking the time left in the week before she and her parents went on vacation, to a house they had rented in Santander. She hadn't seen her father with Sandra again. She'd seen Sandra once, alone, with a grocery bag. Sandra had recognized her by her Doctors Without Borders vest and come up to her.

"Remember me?" she asked.

"Of course."

"I always see you on my way home."

She didn't feel nervous that time, didn't even get flustered at the idea of Sandra having seen her without her realizing it, at having been the one being watched rather than the one doing the watching. Sandra seemed sadder but also sturdier. She was wearing a simple pair of jeans and a T-shirt, and concealer under her eyes, as though she'd drunk too much the night before. Still, she looked fresh and bubbly. She asked if she'd gotten a lot of donations for Doctors Without Borders that day, and Marina said not too many.

"Take down my contact info, if you want, that way at least you'll have one."

She made a small donation. *I'm afraid I'm not a millionaire,* she said by way of an excuse. And without knowing why, as she took down her address and phone number, she was certain that her father had left her. She couldn't have said what that certainty was based on, but she suddenly had no doubt whatsoever; he'd left her, and Sandra hadn't taken it badly, hadn't made a scene, hadn't hounded him, hadn't ever called at four in the morning or sent a text message. It wasn't her style. She'd cried, no doubt, probably berated herself for getting involved with a married man, and that was about it. It must have happened about a week ago,

153

maybe the day she'd gone to her place, maybe a little after that. And now she had the air of the recently dumped, a mix of dignity and dejection. She looked prettier than she herself realized, had a kind of unconscious beauty. She thought she was wearing perfume.

"I don't know my account number by heart," she said.

"You don't need it, here's the Doctors Without Borders account number, you just make a transfer into theirs."

"Oh, right, of course."

"I like your perfume," Marina said.

She'd suddenly felt the need to say something nice, pay her a compliment, any compliment, and that was the first thing she'd thought of.

"Oh, thanks, a friend gave it to me and I can't tell if I like it or not, I almost never wear it. You don't think it's a little strong?"

"No."

"Maybe I'm just not used to it," she laughed, "sometimes I feel like I'm leaving a *trail* of perfume down the street."

"That's how I felt about this cologne my father gave me one time," Marina said, "it would get up in my nose, right here, and go straight to my brain, I thought I'd never be able to smell anything else for the rest of my *life*."

Sandra laughed. She had a strong, confident laugh that somehow rectified her features, as though her face were only complete mid-laugh. It gave her a pleasant, intimate feeling to be talking to Sandra that way, to know that her father had called it off with her, to know that she'd been sad and that she was gradually starting to feel better. Her body had a sort of measured calm about it, like when sick people seem to withdraw into themselves in order to allow their bodies to repair something that's not functioning right inside them; she thought she *got* it.

"You want to buy me a Coke? That way I could take a break, even if it's just for a little while."

Sandra smiled.

"Sure."

She's so lonely, she thought, but not in a pitying way. They walked side by side a little way and then sat at an outdoor café. Not for long, maybe fifteen minutes. Sandra had to go, she was meeting someone. *Liar*, she thought, but liked that she was lying, liked that the lie had a familiar air. They talked—about what? It didn't matter. Words were exchanged and replies were given, the small talk of those on merely polite terms. Sandra talked about the newspaper where she worked, and she pretended not to know and to find it fascinating, confessed that she wanted to be a writer, said she was going to write her first novel that summer, spoke to her about the lake where time stood still, about the characters—making them up then and there— and suddenly, also then and there, had a brilliant idea: she quickly concocted a character, a married man who was unfaithful to his wife. Sandra didn't bat an eye.

"Do you want to hear something that would make a good story?" Sandra asked.

"Sure."

"It's about a friend of mine who had an affair with a married man."

Sandra slid down until their knees were almost touching, a somewhat strained position she then adjusted by scooting back and recrossing her legs. She seemed to be searching for the proper way to position her body in order to tell the story, and to be unable to find it, like a boxer before a fight. She didn't seem sad, more teasing, like she was dancing around an image.

"My friend knew from the start that he was a married man, and she also knew that he was no snake. Maybe a bit vain, but no snake, and very good-looking. They met at the office. At first he didn't even try to flirt with her, he'd just be there, looking at her, and she assumed he was attracted to her, but he really wasn't, not at all. One day after work, they went to have a drink. He talked a lot. My friend thought he was a little old, but she liked him, she'd just moved to Madrid and she didn't know anyone. They ended up getting involved. They'd see each other when they could, almost always at my friend's house, almost always after work. He never talked about his wife. One time, my friend asked him about her, and all he said was that he loved her. Anyway, one night, they'd just finished making love, and he started doing this thing, started stroking her eyebrows. It was this simple thing, silly, really—he traced the tip of his index finger along her eyebrow, from one end to the other. And all of the sudden, for some reason, she felt sick to her stomach. There was something about that little gesture that made her sick."

"Why?"

"At first she wasn't sure. It just made her sick. He'd take his index finger and trace the length of her eyebrow, really slowly. Then, suddenly, it dawned on her. That was something he did with his wife. Does that make sense?"

"Yes."

"It was an expression of intimacy, *someone else's* intimacy, something he did with his wife when they made love. My friend told him never to touch her that way again. And then suddenly their whole affair made her sick. What do you think? You think you could make a story out of *that*?"

"I don't know."

"Give it a try, *I* think it would make a great story."

"It's a pretty good story."

"I have to go," Sandra said, rising and picking up the change from the bill. "I'll see you around soon, I guess."

"Actually, you won't. I'm going on vacation with my family."

"Oh, lucky you."

"I know, we're going to Comillas, in Santander."

"That's great."

Suddenly they were both uncomfortable, both wanted to get away. Sandra gave her a light, halfhearted kiss on the cheek, the kind of kiss you give a second cousin, and after they said goodbye, Marina pretended to be walking back to the Plaza Callao and then turned around to watch her one last time. She had a crisp, determined walk. Her perfume hung in the air. It smelled like some kind of water flower. Something thick and verdant.

The house was on the outskirts of town, and it was magnificent. An old manor house, twenty minutes from the beach. They brought five suitcases, four full of clothes and one full of books. Her father made the most of his summers, reading classics and other hefty volumes he didn't have time for during the year. Marina thought all three of them seemed more pensive than usual on the drive up. Her father and mother got into an argument because her mother forgot to buy a bottle of water when they stopped at a gas station, and their squabbling dragged on for almost an hour. From the back seat, she watched her father's tense hands gripping the steering wheel, and half of each of their faces, split by the rearview mirror. They rarely argued, maybe that was why they both found it so hard to give in when they did. Marina thought her mother seemed to be getting stupider, had become virtually incapable of reasoning, and that her father had fallen into an exasperating loop, simply repeating the same argument over and over. The bickering began afresh when they got to town and couldn't find the road that the rental house was on. Finally they arrived, in such foul moods that all three of them would have turned around and gone straight back to Madrid had anyone suggested it. *Aren't you ever going to forgive me?* Ramón texted.

The first three days were hard; it was as though, upon waking, they donned invisible shackles and obeyed some command, like an arduous obligation—the vacationers' to-do list, the trips to the beach, the grilled sardines at lunch, the Cantabrian bowling in the afternoon. Her father devoted himself almost entirely to his books, and her mother made her play sidekick when she went out to buy *sobao* cakes and Santoña anchovies. But the house they'd rented was so pleasant that it began to have a mysterious effect on them, a favorable effect. At first they hardly realized. They were not a loud bunch, didn't talk much. When they did, their conversations sometimes had a slightly schizophrenic feel, as though each of them, independently from one another, were periodically relaying an unrelated series of isolated thoughts. It seemed like the house had secret passageways linking them together almost against their will. After four days, something in them loosened. Sometimes they would catch themselves staring at one another without realizing it, and then they smiled, sort of dreamily.

"We'll never be able to come back here. This place is so wonderful that we can never come back. *It would never be the same*," her mother said. Even her optimism was fatalistic. Her father would laugh, and for a moment, she'd stop seeing the face that had kissed Sandra. She'd see the face of her father, looking somewhat worn, and humbled, and vain, and affable. Suddenly, he showed clear signs of the passage of time, had a different look, vanquished somehow. The way she'd loved him up until then proved unworkable now, like a sunken bridge on a distant continent, or in a fable. He had been born in Santander, lived there until he was eighteen, so being back brought to mind anecdotes that he recounted without warning, when he was mid-chapter, as though they were plaguing him. He would raise his head from his book and say, "I remember one time . . ."

Her mother insisted on planting a little vegetable garden in the yard and threw herself into tending it with the tenacity and impatience that only a city woman can. She would take her cup of tea outside each morning as though secretly hoping that a plant that had nothing on it the day before might today bear a lustrous, ready-to-pick tomato. Marina would go out to help her, and think about Ramón. She thought about him as though out of some physical need, as though being there amid all that tranquility made her body impatient, abruptly aroused. Sometimes, when she got into bed at night, she'd masturbate absentmindedly. She'd suddenly feel cocky and grown-up, as though she were doing an expert job, and through sheer force of will, she'd conjure up the memory of Ramón's head in her hands, which she would take and trap between her legs. Then she'd drift off to sleep in the lovely sway of the breeze coming in through the window, the sound of the breeze in the trees, like a giant, gentle hand caressing the surface of the earth.

One afternoon, she and her father went fishing, just the two of them. They bought a couple of touristy fishing poles and sat out at the marina. Marina caught a tiny fish, silver and twitching. She felt the bite like a muscle tightening and reeled in her line until a tiny bream appeared, the size of a saucer. It thrashed its little tail and opened and closed its mouth with mesmerizing anxiety. In order to pull it from the water and help her free it from the hook, her father wrapped his arms around her, and she felt his weight. She got so panicky, and her father took so long, that by the time they tossed it back into the water, it was already dead. It just floated there, one tiny, vertical eye staring up at the sky. They pretended not to see it, but the current kept dragging it back to them, over and over again. Marina thought, for the first time, *I'm going to tell him right now, I'll tell him I know everything.* She was tormented by the urge, an urge that had never existed until that moment, as though she needed desperately to become an adult, or an accomplice, in the eyes of her father, and the mere prospect of doing it made her so nervous that she was paralyzed and silent for several minutes.

"I remember when I was nineteen, just before I moved to Madrid, I had a love affair right here in this town," her father said.

She turned to face him. He had the same far-off look he'd been getting when he told a story those days. It wasn't the first time she'd heard him talk about an old lover. In her family, both her father and mother would occasionally bring up former boyfriends and girlfriends with an absentminded lack of restraint, as though it didn't matter in the slightest, as though it were amusing to paint a vaguely humiliating portrait of them.

"She was a small-town girl, really pretty, a little shy. What was her name . . .?"

Her father stared silently at the little floating fish for a few seconds, as though perhaps it might respond, from the dead.

"For some reason, I told her I wanted to marry her. Then when I got back to Santander, a few days before I was going to Madrid, the whole thing suddenly seemed absurd. I was too ashamed to call her and tell her I didn't love her, just like that. So I wrote a letter, telling her I had a disease, a terrible skin condition, something really unpleasant, and that I was going to die soon, that there was nothing that could be done."

He fell silent again, smiling, as though he were about to burst out laughing.

"What was her name . . .?" he asked the fish once more.

"So what happened?"

"I went to Madrid. When I'd been there two weeks, your grandmother called. She told me that a girl had turned up at the house, in Santander, asking for me. And

161

that she'd said she didn't care about the disease, it didn't matter to her . . . What do you think of that?"

"I don't know."

"Isn't it sweet?"

"Yeah."

"I suddenly pictured her leaving home, this shy girl . . . I don't know, getting on a bus, going all the way to Santander, showing up and introducing herself to my mother . . ."

They bought some nice white wine, and seafood to have with it, and went back to the house. At dinner they hardly spoke, and they drank an entire bottle of wine before they'd started eating, and another as they ate. Her mother put on some music. Her father seemed to be in high spirits after the story of the girl who'd fallen in love with him. Marina's memory of that night was vague, as though the whole of it were somehow muted—the sound of the breeze across the yard, her mother's summer dress, the smell of after-sun lotion. She remembered that her father had poured a whisky for himself, and then one for her, and that her mother had pretended to be scandalized. She remembered that they went to bed without cleaning up and that she had heard the two of them laugh that night, in their room, and then a bit later heard the sound of her mother going out to the bathroom, which was down the hall, and then closing the bedroom door. Then brief whispering. And later there'd been another foray into the bathroom by her father, or her mother. Next came a troubling silence, during which she knew with unquestionable certainty that they were getting undressed. She recalled that she stopped focusing on the book she was reading and "opened" her ears. The noises she heard sounded almost cruel, in a way, as though one of the two of them were deliberately hurting the other a little, then came a sort of cacophonous melody, somehow offbeat, and then suddenly, unmistakably sharp—like a freakish tropical bird, cawing in the middle of the night—her mother gasping, and a shrill little laugh.

The following morning, after she woke, she walked drowsily down the hall, and as she passed her parents' door, she saw that it was ajar. It wasn't the first time she'd seen them sleeping, but when she did, she nearly always felt a sort of awkward prudishness that made her look the other way or hurry past. That morning, too, she hurried past, went to the bathroom and then to the kitchen, but the smell of unwashed dishes and seafood from the night before made her so sick that she decided to go back to bed and read so her mother would be the one to clean it up. On her way back down the hall, she passed their slightly open door once more, and that time she stopped. She silently pushed it a little further open, trying not to make any noise, and instantly became flustered.

She wanted to see.

She wanted to blush.

She, too, wanted to do something cruel and intimate.

And to open that door, to stare shamelessly.

At first, she couldn't really see anything. She had to stand there leaning against the doorjamb, waiting for her eyes to adjust to the darkness. It took a few minutes. She could hear them breathing, though. It was like a conversation between friends who are slightly irritated with one another, one responding kindly to the other's

163

outbursts; she heard her mother's low whistle first and then, immediately after, her father's emphatic snore.

She was gradually able to see them clearly.

They were deep in slumber, her father face down in his underwear, head under his pillow, her mother leaning toward her father, summer nightgown tangled between her legs. They looked ragged, amiable, exhausted, as though something had been tossing them around in the air all night, above the bed, and then just dropped them there in those positions. The air in the room was stale. It smelled of sleep. A tremor passed over them, moving through their bodies. They bore a physical resemblance, like siblings. Her mother had one hand under her pillow and the other reaching out to her father's leg, as though she couldn't sleep without touching him, without knowing he was still there. There was a rustling, something that seemed to come from the sound of their breathing itself, mysteriously syncopated. Her father lifted his head slightly and turned it toward her mother, lurching and turning onto his side, his knees leaning against her hip. Marina instantly feared that her father might wake up all of the sudden and catch her spying on them, but he settled once more and stopped moving. It was a dance, a slow and boundless dance, each of them so at the mercy of the other that everything around them seemed provisional. It was only her presence that made the things around them real—the lightbulb hanging from the ceiling, the nightstand, yesterday's clothes on the little armchair by the sideboard, the newspaper that her father had brought up to read in bed and then not read, the ashtray with the butt of the last cigarette her mother had smoked—from all of those things seeped a presence that was contained and concentrated in their bodies. Up until now, she'd assumed that it was for fear of seeing their nakedness, albeit accidentally, that she was embarrassed to watch her parents sleep, now she understood that what she was really afraid of, what she was ashamed of, was something else; it was as though something had altered their intimacy itself. She felt like she'd never truly seen them before.

She closed the door as slowly as she could, trying to make as little noise as possible, and not until she heard the little click that meant it was all the way shut did she realize how nervous she was. She thought it was astonishing that week in and week out, for more years than she'd been alive, the striking scene she'd just witnessed was repeated daily. Something about that feeling reminded her vaguely of that Dylan Thomas quote, that letter he'd written his girlfriend, or wife, maybe, she didn't know which. She sat on the chair in her room, looked out at the chestnut tree in all its splendor. It had rained a little in the night, and when she opened the window, a cool, fresh scent wafted in. She took out a few pieces of paper, sat down somewhat theatrically, and wrote as neatly as she could:

> *"You mustn't look too grown up, because you'd look older than me; and you'll never, I'll never let you, grow wise, and I'll never, you shall never let me, grow wise, and we'll always be young and unwise together."*

SHOPPING

As she's waiting for Nelly on the corner of the Plaza Colón, it begins to snow outside. An ill-defined flurry, tentative at first, then heavy for nearly five minutes, then tentative once more. Snow in Madrid. People get momentarily excited, despite the irritability brought on by Christmas shopping and the cold, and they suddenly act a bit childish. Snow always infantilizes people, she thinks. Snow always infantilizes, and Nelly always turns up late—ten minutes late, fifteen. Snow also has its own peculiar sound, like a plane flying overhead in the distance, and its own peculiar grace, the way it dissolves almost instantly on the sidewalk. The sky is blanketed in a bright, almost blinding white, as though the sunlight had thundered across the entire expanse of sky and filtered down in crystallized form, tiny glints ricocheting off Madrileños' heads. Voices ring out, "Snow, snow," in different pitches, almost all of them children's. Voices, and a silent crackling, as though someone had imposed silence. Finally, she spots Nelly, flawless in a brown, three-quarter-length coat, on the other side of the Calle Serrano, hair pulled back and lips painted their customary fire-engine red. Why has she never called her *Mamá*? Perhaps, quite simply, because it's impossible to call someone like Nelly *Mamá*, perhaps because she herself forbade it when she was a little girl. *Don't call me Mamá, call me by my name—call me Nelly.* She can't recall the conversation, but she's sure it must have taken place. *What's this "Mamá" business?* She remembers always having called her Nelly, remembers, distinctly, the astonishment of the other girls at school who called their mothers *Mamá*, and the sense—which has cemented over the years—of how inappropriate it was ever, at any point in her life, to have thought that Nelly could possibly be called anything but Nelly, even by the likes of her own daughter.

Nelly gives a curt wave to indicate that she's seen her, then turns back to face the traffic on Serrano. It's always the same with Nelly—everything takes place all around her, it's as if she gave off a strange, dramatic perfume. She hasn't seen her in nearly four months, since the funeral, and she looks prettier now, more at peace, maybe. Her beauty is a gift. There are millions of women who would kill to look like Nelly at fifty-six, and Nelly knows it, which is why she acts, at times, as though beauty were an inconsequential and somewhat silly concern; she communicates as much in each of her gestures, in the way she won't turn her head toward her, keeps looking out at the traffic, as though the person she were on her way to meet were standing there and not on the other side of the street and she were observing them, unseen. Or as though something had somehow obstructed her train of thought and she'd turned her head away from the distraction. Suddenly she feels ashamed at not having put more effort into her appearance, dressed up more to go shopping with Nelly. Stepping out of the shower, she'd considered it, knowing that exactly this situation would arise, but in the end, she decided on a pair of jeans, boots, and a run-of-the-mill coat. It was a small act of vengeance. *I'm not dressing up just for her*, she thought and pulled on her jeans with a slightly absurd sense of triumph. She left home feeling attractive and gradually lost confidence as she made her way to the corner, where she arrived with none at all. As always, she sought to comfort herself, repeating over and over that it really didn't matter, yet glancing at her reflection in storefront windows at every possible opportunity. What she saw there was a thirty-year-old with a mother's figure, a slightly scruffy air, a face that was pretty but too full, boots that didn't go with her jeans, and an unconvincing walk; every time she saw herself, she had the urge to say, *That is not me.* She feels it more now than ever, as the light turns red and Nelly heads toward her.

"It's ridiculous, this snow," she says, giving her a kiss. "Can you believe it?"

"I know."

To hope that Nelly might apologize for being late would be asking too much, so she doesn't. But she's angry with herself and struggling to be pleasant. She's thinking that they have to go Christmas shopping for her aunts and that it's going to be a long day. A long day with Nelly.

"It's always the same when it snows in Madrid, three measly flakes and everything is total chaos, that's what I said to Rafael on my way out."

Rafael is Nelly's husband, a banker she met three years ago and only ever brings up as a phantom interlocutor when what she really wants is to repeat something she said earlier. "He's the perfect husband," she says, "hardly ever speaks." They got married two years ago, and she remembers the wedding, remembers Nelly in the hotel room in Santander, putting on the finishing touches, remembers Papá's phone calls (*How's everything going up north?*), his faux-polite voice sounding strangely wounded (*Does your mother look pretty?*), Nelly's swagger—*How do I look? Are you impressed?* She also remembers standing by Nelly's side, suddenly sensing an abrupt distance, the smell of the flowers in her hair, a smell that seemed like it was from her childhood but wasn't, Nelly's implacable presence, the rain that began to splatter against the windows (*Please tell me it's not going to start raining right now*) and then immediately stopped, giving way to a glorious day, full of just-washed freshness.

"So, what do you think, where should we start?"

"I don't know, wherever you want."

"What's the matter? It's like you're not even here."

"No, I'm fine, it's just that I almost froze waiting for you out here."

"Well, you should have waited in a café."

There couldn't have been a more Nelly reply, she thinks. She has a knack for repackaging things so that if anyone tries to reproach her, she turns the whole thing immediately, blisteringly on its head. The reproach, as ever, now rebounds onto her. Of course she could have waited in a café, that's not the issue. The issue is, quite simply, that Nelly was *late*. And perhaps there's another issue, too—the fact that she's smiling against her will, that she can picture her smile as if she were standing at a mirror—wounded,

170

ambiguous, manipulated by Nelly, a bit dim-witted, like the faint, dopey smile of her father, but without his good will, a smile that fails to strike a tone. *I can't rescue every broken-winged bird*, Nelly likes to say. As well as, *You're impossible, kid, just like your father, I can never tell what either of you think of me.*

"We could start with Aunt Mariana," she finally says.

"Yes," replies Nelly, "she's the easiest."

With Nelly, you never know if *easy* is a virtue or a character flaw. In any case, for her, it's neither. She's always considered natural behavior the most arduous and least natural battle a woman has to wage. Sometimes she even believes that acting natural is simply the most sophisticated of orthopedics, a vague cumulus of rehearsed expressions, expressions that eventually become reflexes by dint of repetition. Not so for Nelly. Nelly is natural like a typhoon is natural, like all true self-centered egotists, like a disaster, like the Grand Canyon, like a luxury item ensconced in an absurdly minimalist display case in a glittery shop window. That's why she heads straight to Loewe, as though there were no need to explain the decision she's come to in her head.

"Initials. Don't let me forget, we have to tell them to monogram her initials."

"On what?"

"A purse."

"I didn't know you could ask them to do that."

"*Of course* you can. They should offer to do it in *gold*."

They walk into the store, and Nelly immediately makes a face.

"I see the place has been remodeled," she says, looking like she just got a stomach cramp.

"Yes," the shop assistant replies solicitously, "we just unveiled the new space three weeks ago."

"My sincere condolences."

The salesclerk smiles. A startled-pigeon smile, quick and fake, as though someone had jabbed his cheeks with two fishhooks and quickly jerked them up. Against all odds, out of sheer nervousness, he responds, "Thank you."

"You're welcome."

She might be the only one who has the right to laugh at Nelly's sense of humor. That, in fact, might be the one thing that has truly filtered down into her own character. It's an expression that seems to begin in the eyebrows, a vague and infinitesimal contracting of the brows that gradually spreads across her whole face, concealing it, like a clever boy who's mischievously sadistic and takes full advantage of how innocent he looks. Humor, for Nelly, is a sign of authority. And detached intimacy—she can't explain it any better than that, can't *conceive* of it any better than that, like with so many other things about Nelly. She remembers many of her jokes, the way she says *charming* every time something horrifies her, the way she lifts her chin just slightly and opens her mouth, feigning surprise, and speaks to the person she's joking with but without addressing them directly, as though humor had to be unusually oblique, a triple bank shot.

"Spain is the epitome of pretense," she quips, glancing at the shop's décor, and then heads to the purses. She looks at them, too. There are some truly beautiful ones with exorbitant price tags, tragic in their luxury. Why has she always found luxury tragic? She's not sure. It's like a facet of her conscience, a sort of decadent, slightly harsh truth, a routine experience that, for some unknown reason, she's never been able to get used to. Again, not so for Nelly. Luxury, for her mother, has always been a sumptuous, kindred thing, a sort of soundtrack to her life that she pays no attention to, or listens to only distractedly, something exceptional and concrete—club insignias, a Corot in the living room (*You have no idea how glad I am I never sold that painting*), a closet full of colorful shoes like a nest of hungry birds. And order, above all, an infantile order, a blind order that infiltrates her childhood memories of Nelly, pervading everything, as though it were part of her own character despite being contingent upon others—never returning home to find the azaleas on the terrace anything but impeccable (*No roses, dear God, that flower is just a mouth inside a mouth inside another mouth*), never having to speak of love, only take it for granted.

"Loewe is like a doting but dull husband," Nelly says without turning to face her, "don't you think?"

"Mm," she smiles.

"Which of these two do you like best? The brown?" And she models, hanging it from her left arm. "Or the black?" And hangs it from the right. Then she does an ill-defined little dance in front of the enormous mirror, left to right, this profile, that profile, glancing at herself more than anything, although also—vaguely and sidelong—at the purses in question. She uses this as an opportunity to examine her carefully for the first time. She hasn't seen her since the funeral, hasn't seen her in four months. She reflects on that again. She's spoken to her two or three times on the phone, but hasn't seen her. It's true that she looks more at peace, and it's true that she seems to have recovered that delicacy of hers, that physically delicate quality Nelly has that's almost sexual, or at least turns her into a sophisticated sex object. She only realized it a few years ago, but this quality of Nelly's is what drives men wild and has for as long as she can remember, is what must have driven Papá wild (no, that's not true, Papá was *different*), and that intimidating lover she had, and the current handsome banker, so like any other potential banker, and the others she never heard about but knows existed.

"The brown."

"Really? I'd say the black," Nelly responds. "The brown is too pedestrian."

"Maybe."

"You're right, though, she could use the brown one more."

Is that a tribute to her opinion or a demerit? She's not sure. Is it a value judgment on Aunt Mariana? Should they be practical, for once, and pick the everyday purse over the pretty purse and thus renounce all that has been, or should they, from now until the end of time, over and above all practicalities, always pick the pretty and unusable purse, the black purse, the perverse and untouchable symbol of desire? *Who do you love the most?* And her little-girl reply: *Who I love the most is . . . Nelly.* A declaration of love. She wondered if her private English tutor later told Nelly what she'd said. *Who I love the most . . . (I will not stand for dirty smocks, or scraps of paper on the floor, or messes, or sticky sofas).* In the mirror of her childhood, she is spellbound, and the spell is now complete, as though a ball tossed into the air when she was six still hadn't come down. Had her tutor told her? Had she not? She hadn't. She had. The mirror of her childhood reflects a woman who both is and is not this Nelly. Something is missing, like a proverb no one bothers to finish because everyone knows how it goes; there's the Christmas decorations, and the freakish snow flurry over Madrid, and the hustle and bustle of people out Christmas shopping, and Papá has died obediently—is that's what changed? Papá, obedient now in death?

"The black, end of discussion."

But there had been no discussion. Only the salesclerk, who's been at her side the whole time and, as Nelly hands him the black purse, says, "If I may, madam, offer my opinion . . ."

"Of course."

"I think you made the *perfect* choice."

When they leave Loewe, snow is no longer falling timidly over Madrid, and all that's left is the cold. She feels young and strangely old at the same time. She's only thirty. She has a nice body—but not too nice, a bit heavyset—a gullible, childlike air, needy, and a way of not understanding life and the world around her that gives her more in common with the people walking past her on the Calle Serrano than with Nelly; it's as though her thoughts were always one step behind her actions. She's too slow, she thinks, never sees anything coming. That which was a virtue in her father is a defect in her. But, like Nelly, she does have a twisted, dangerous quality, something hidden in the shadows of a back room.

"What do you say, should we walk up to the Plaza de la Independencia and then come back down? I'd like to stop by Sybilla, I want to treat myself to a little something, and maybe there will be something pretty for you there, too."

"Sure."

With Nelly, there's never much need to talk. Not even when she was six and Nelly left home was there much need to talk. She remembers the living room in their apartment, now rented out, and the creaking parquet floor, the lonely-girl game she played with each creak (*Captain, it's sinking, our ship is sinking*)—it was comforting to imagine that a storm might hit Madrid and flood the streets all the way up to the fourth floor (they lived on the fifth), that she would be able to jump out the window and into the water; then suddenly she sees her father's profile, the living room, two coffee cups and, on one of them, Nelly's lips (Nelly's spellbinding lips stamped on cups, cigarettes, Papá's cheek, next to his lips, almost at the corner of his lips, as though everything she touched were somehow branded). *I'm going to go away for a while, kid.* The scene suddenly has a certain mystique to it, as though it's been slathered with a layer of shiny varnish—Nelly gesturing, her father motionless. *Come now, don't cry, I'm not going off to live on the other side of the world.* Was that tasteless, or was it not? The lover, the leaving home, the taxi awaiting Nelly (the two of them were, in fact, going off, but to London)—suddenly it all seems tasteless and fictional, the skeleton of a scene from a bad, sappy movie. But her love is no skeleton. Her love is reborn every day. She and Papá often sit in the living room—he with a whisky and a blank stare, she playing dead, not blinking, picturing everyone gathering around her and screaming, terrified, *She's dead, she's dead!* and she herself motionless, cloistered inside her own body, laughing to herself (*You won't be happy until your liver rots, until it turns to mush, is that it, Antonio?*); they don't take Nelly's photos down, how could they? Their love is a spellbound expanse, their game, slightly deranged. She remembers the two of them talking about Nelly almost every day—how pretty she is, how much they love her, how much they miss her, whether or not she's going to come back. She's not sure whether she becomes an adult or her father becomes a child in those conversations, all she knows is that they keep the fires burning, the fires in the temple of Nelly-love, and that neither of them can help it. It's only now, twenty-five years later, that she sees it was lunacy to have played such a game with a little girl, but she doesn't hold it against him. It's like having witnessed and enabled someone else's weakness, simply because it coincides with your own. Sometimes a postcard arrives or the telephone rings and it's *her*. Then her heart pounds furiously, she can't speak, she gives monosyllabic responses to everything. *Is that all the happy you are to hear from me?*

"You're so quiet today."

"Yeah, well . . ."

"The initials."

"What?"

"We forgot to have them monogram her initials."

"Oh, right."

"Let's go to Sybilla first, then stop in again on the way back."

"How do they do it?" she finally asks. It's the first genuine question she's managed to ask all day.

"The monogram? With heat, I imagine. The purses are leather, so it must be like branding a horse."

How extraordinary, how apt those words suddenly seem—*branding a horse.* Is it surprising that they still haven't spoken about Papá? Of course not, but when she left home, she thought for a second that *today* they finally would, that it would come up naturally in conversation. They've never spoken about him in any serious way, and now he's dead, so isn't it about time? But she wouldn't even know where to begin, sadly; the enormity of the topic is such that there could only be vast, generic, open-ended questions—*Why?* Questions that no doubt Nelly would find in poor taste to answer—*What do you mean, why? Why what?* How long was she away from Madrid? A year? More? And the whole time in London. In her memory, London took on the form of a chosen city, a glimmering paradise, because Nelly was there. The postcards that arrived every once in a while, addressed to her, all had that bright, emblematic London red on them someplace, a red so like Nelly's lips. *Here I am, kid, this is an amazing city.* And her little-girl game: covering the rest of the sentence and reading, again and again, *here I am,* turning over the postcard, seeing Hyde Park; *here I am,* turning over the postcard, seeing Battle Abbey; *here I am,* turning over the postcard, seeing the London phone booth her mother might have called her from; *here I am,* turning over the postcard, seeing a string of plasticky clouds and an ivy-covered cottage in the shady background; *here I am; here I am; here I am.* Now, not then, imagining Nelly with that lover (*A son-of-the-count-of-something-or-other*); from their window, they could see migratory birds, Papá knew what almost all of them were—storks, herons, ducks—planning all the things she'd tell Nelly when she called, writing them all down on a piece of paper (*Sofía didn't invite me to her party; I lost a tooth, it fell out at school, at lunch, and I almost swallowed it; We went to the zoo and the thing I liked best was the dolphins)*, her mind racing through the conversation she'd worked out in advance, the things she'd say to her, the thrill of almost having swallowed but not swallowing her tooth, the electrified, almost humiliating indignation of not having been at Sofía's party, the dolphins' iridescent skin, saving for last the fact that they'd been allowed to touch them, describing what it felt like, so unexpected, so plastic, so detached, but her real voice choked on the words, her real voice and the clear, slightly gravelly sound of Nelly's voice in the distance, in London, brought out her monosyllabic replies. *Is that all the happy you are to hear my voice?*

"I haven't been to Sybilla in *eons*. Do you think that sweet salesgirl still works there?"

"I don't know."

Nelly moves close, takes her arm. She switches the bag holding their first purchase to the other side, to make herself more comfortable. She feels the touch of Nelly's body against her own, the contact of Nelly's hip against her own, her whole leg, almost, keeping stride with her. For a second, they walk in silence. For a second, Madrid seems beautiful. More than beautiful—deferrable. As though that were the most agreeable, most lovable quality a city could have, the most genteel quality, that of being deferrable. And there's another quality, too: suppleness. Everything seems as though it could sink into Madrid, into that yawning stomach, and be absorbed and digested, even a stone. The cold confers a peculiar beauty on the faces of the passersby, makes them taut and pure, as though they were marble, as though they had been very finely buffed. She doesn't think of herself as more intelligent or happier than any of those people. She thinks, in fact, that she's not very intelligent, that she's not very happy, that perhaps she's not even good, but she's tired of constantly conjecturing about herself— I'm this, I'm that. Since Papá died, she's hardly even read a book, hardly gone out; the only thing she does, the only thing she wants to do—though she wouldn't tell Nelly for anything in the world—is make love. Fuck. She's been doing it these past four months with one ex-boyfriend and one lover, a married man who calls when he can and shows up at her door with a hungry look, spends the obligatory quarter of an hour talking to her, and then proceeds to undress her right there in the kitchen, in the bathroom. It's almost better with him than with the ex-boyfriend. The other day, they were doing it, and out of the blue, he just spat in her face, and then she spat on his, and they spat on each other for a while without knowing why, and she felt the urge to be hurt, an urge as seductive and pulsating as failure, and she came three times, and when they were done, after he left, she wanted to call him and beg him to come back and fuck her again, fuck her all afternoon. It was terrible and lighthearted and fragile and surprising all at once to see the way an unexpected action led to an unexpected surge of solemn, electrifying feelings, trapped inside themselves like capsules. Sometimes, she liked for it to hurt a little. Sometimes, she liked to take it up the ass. She liked to feel another person's hunger, first anxious and then intent on its own gratification; she liked behavior that seemed destructive and then became caring, and then destructive again, digging in its heels with a frenzied

180

determination to *get* something and then dissolving as though it had never existed, leaving only the desire to do it all over again, anew. Every repetition was proof of defeat and proof of success; she stopped thinking about Papá, about Nelly, and she felt the way these people passing her on the street were feeling now—cold, beautiful, unable to resolve anything but full of desires—the people of Madrid, laden with bags, laden with expectations. Is it the contact of Nelly's arm that makes her pity them all? Though it's not really pity, just as the contact of Nelly's arm is not only contact. It's an *expanse*. The sidewalk on the Calle Serrano is an expanse, and the sight of the Puerta de Alcalá, off in the distance, and the tinkling in people's eyes, and the snippets of Christmas carols that can be heard when a shop door opens here and there—it's like catching only one bit of a conversation in which someone suddenly says *a babe is born*.

"The mayor has absolutely lost it," Nelly says, referring to the construction work. "The other day, a friend of Rafael's from Paris said to me, 'Madrid is a charming city, but it will be even more so when they finally find the treasure.'"

Nelly turns to her, amused, as though needing to explain the joke to her.

"You know, buried treasure."

"Well, at least all the drilling drowns out the sound of the Christmas carols," she retorts, because she knows Nelly will like that joke.

"Don't be so sure, Christmas carols are emitted at their own unique frequency, they're *indestructible*. My idea of hell is a record stuck on 'The Little Drummer Boy'."

Finally, she makes her smile. Nelly, she now knows—though she only recently figured this out—has a truly sexual quality about her when she laughs. For many years, Nelly's sex life has been a mystery to her, and she's only gotten a glimpse of certain events, milestones: the lover she left Papá for, another man she saw with her several times, a friend of her father's who was constantly admiring her beauty, her current husband, the ridiculously naïve and ridiculously handsome banker. How many men have there been in Nelly's life? She thinks of Aunt Mariana's advice: *If you want to know how many men a woman has had, make a reasonable guess, and then add five.* Looking at any one part of Nelly is like looking at all of her, her whole body, there's always some sort of sound that interrupts her gaze, a sound that *is* her body, and her body is indisputable, but does not project itself in any one direction in particular. In her mind, she calls up some of the sexual looks Nelly has given men; they seem out of context now, and back then she didn't know what kind of looks they were, but *now* she gets it. Nelly's sexual look is the same as the smile a woman gives a grocer when he quotes her a price that's too high—it's like a sharp fluttering in her cheeks, or her eyelids, a note of suspicion and premonition, and perhaps of commitment. It's like sex is something Nelly owes to no one but herself, something unrelated to anybody else in particular, which is why she and no one else—and maybe Nelly knows this, though most likely she's never even stopped to consider it—is the only person capable of truly picturing her in certain positions, doing certain things. No, not even the men she's been with, the men who have *seen her*. No, not even Papá. And she's also convinced that she's been misinterpreted. And she is sure of this: there is something Nelly doesn't like about herself, something *physical*, she can feel it, like something she can put her hand on and stroke, something that over the course of a very long time has faded like a distant memory, or like a defect that first leads to a hang-up, then to anxiety, then indifference, then pride, and then nothing.

"I love Madrid in the winter, Madrid is a winter city," Nelly says.

Something, perhaps the Christmas carol joke, has put her in a good mood. Nelly's good moods always require a counterpoint, it's the fulcrum on which her social self rests. And she knows exactly what is required of her in order to encourage this mood: disagreement.

"No," she replies, "it's a spring city."

"Don't be ridiculous, *every city* is a spring city."

"No, wait," she fires back immediately, "I know what Madrid's season is: September to November, early autumn, that's when Madrid really comes to life."

Nelly takes a few steps in silence. She feels her pull away slightly, then lean back in, feels the reverberating contact of Nelly's arm once more, slightly tense. She turns to her.

"You know what, you're absolutely right."

What a strange sense of triumph—Nelly, conceding a point, what unexpected allegiance. She even repeats it.

"*Absolutely right*, I'd never thought of that before."

Why is this little triumph not making her happier? It seems to fade immediately, as though, for a second, she no longer wanted to feel Nelly's arm resting on hers. She hates that about herself, the way she can be upbeat and then deflated one second later, over any stupid little thing.

Desires fulfilled yield sadness, rather than happiness, for her. It was different for Papá—despite his illness, his attention was always focused on Nelly like a bright, unceasing light. Maybe that's why Nelly left him, she thinks now, because he'd made her life the only purpose of his own. Now she sees that it's hard to bear *being loved* unfailingly, regardless of logic, regardless of merit. Being adored is exhausting. *I am who I am, you know that, I've never tried to hide anything,* Nelly says; and once, two years ago, *Your father sometimes thinks that everybody can go around gushing with love, morning, noon and night, like him.* She remembers that the comment really stung and then immediately stopped stinging—like accidentally touching an open sore—when she took into account that a virtue can also be a defect if you just shift your perspective a few inches. But perhaps she misjudged something, she thinks, and not just Nelly—herself, too. It's strange, but she thinks she can sense an impending intuition, right this minute, she's about to have it, about to hit on something she's never hit on before. And stranger still, her brain has already intuited it but not yet dared to articulate it. Suddenly, it does: *Papá knew.* The thought is achingly simple—the suede shoes, the ring he'd had special ordered from a jeweler in Denmark, the rug with different shades of red, his job as an architect, the Maupassant novels he liked to read, *he knew it,* and the Sunday crossword (his only confessable vice aside from alcohol), he knew from the start that Nelly was going to leave him, knew that it was only a matter of time. The thought follows the strange trajectory of thoughts that have been had many times but never fully grasped. Now she thinks she understands— he knew it *from the start,* the way the rabbit knows upon entering the lion's cage that it is going to be devoured, so when the first bite comes, it does not whimper, does not squeal, does not make any sound at all, though it cannot help but cower and flail from side to side. The terrible thing about the rabbit is not that it lets itself be eaten but rather its silence, the smile on its wan lips, its turtledove manner, its near-total lack of offense, and, even worse, the absolute knowledge that all of those things thwart any hope of ever being loved by the lion again (*Does your mother ever talk about me?*), and that is why the rabbit cowers, in his only real act of valor—that of having entered the cage to begin with—and ends up trapped there (*Are you trying to prove something, Antonio, drinking like that?*), doesn't betray the slightest sign, doesn't fall down, doesn't die, doesn't change; his lack of resistance is his victory, an uncalculated victory (*Your mother looks lovely this evening, doesn't she?*), and the rest of the time, his attention remains focused like a spotlight on Nelly (*She never talks about me, does she?*), he comes home, shows no sign of neediness but does need complicity, needs for her to accompany him in his love of the lion, needs an accomplice to his insanity, and finds it in his little girl.

When they walk into Sybilla, she immediately revels in the heating, although the warmth, combined with her distressing realization, causes her to give an ambiguous shiver. Nelly lets go of her arm as soon as they enter the boutique and strides to the counter. Immediately, she asks, "Does that girl still work here . . . what was her name?"

Like all good egotists, all utterly spirited women, Nelly possesses this defect: she forever thinks that everyone knows

185

exactly what she's talking about, as though whatever it was that impressed or seduced her were cause for universal impression or seduction.

"You mean Diana?"

"Maybe."

"She's not here anymore."

"What a shame, that girl was a *doll*."

She, too, loves this boutique, the obsession and the lassitude it produces, the absentminded, covetous touch of the fabrics, the sight of the racks hung first with dresses, then shirts, and then skirts, the antique mannequin, the ochre tones, the parquet floor, the smell of the dresses. Each fabric has its own distinct scent, but in the tiny boutique, they all blend together, like a room that's been slept in. It's like entering a personal paradise, one constructed slowly and carefully, something that's been rehearsed over the course of several months of trials and errors, until finally it's all laid out with great simplicity by someone who understands that the insignificant things are the only ones that really matter, that excitement is built on others' transgressions, and that the power of any rhythm or order is, in fact, a courtship. Evening gowns, dresses that change your life, shirts that seem to have been designed expressly for you at some point before the world began—they *always* look bad on hangers. For a second, she forgets Nelly; it's a pleasant feeling. She forgets her and enters her own private avarice. The dresses that change your life, that turn into second skins, can only ever be recognized once on the body, never on the hanger. That is the simultaneously unheroic yet erotic reality of these dresses. She loves the perverse surge of power that suddenly shoots through her, like a jolt of electricity, the allure, the siren's song of the feel of the fabric, not like love but like an impulse and like a flush of feeling, like a burn, like selfishness, and like the best thing in the world, the best-kept lie in history. Being with Nelly now, four months after Papá's death, brings up feelings from before his death, and she forgets for a second her persistent sense of orphanhood, forgets his sickly contact, scrawny arms, labored breath, the fear, the tormented effort to repress her feelings, and lets herself be carried away.

"Nobody makes evening gowns like Sybilla," Nelly says, holding up a black one. "I think I'm going to try this on. Have you found anything for you?"

"Not yet."

Nelly goes into a changing room and a few minutes later beckons her in. Outside, the sun disappears for a second and then returns. The clothes Nelly was wearing now lie on the bench and Nelly is in a black dress, perhaps too young for her—it has a plunging back, revealing her shoulder blades, and hangs to the top of her knees. She was hoping not to be impressed by Nelly, but she is. What else could she possibly be? She's fought the feeling many times, has hated her, has on occasion proclaimed that she didn't exist, even tried to behave as though she were dead. And all it takes to tear it all down is seeing Nelly for one second in a black dress in a dressing room four months after Papá's death, contemplating her endless face, a face that looks chiseled into shape, with infinite concealments that make it impossible to ever see it clearly.

"What do you think?" Nelly asks without looking at her, gesturing strangely, as though trying to smooth down her hips.

"It looks great on you."

Nelly laughs at herself. A macabre, slightly venomous laugh. There's no sadness in it, but there is an undulating silkiness that seems to have been previously kept in check and now seeps into that little cave, into the intimacy of the changing room. If she let herself, she might actually be jealous of her, of her body, her way of taking love for granted, her resolve, her awareness. There, beneath that dress, stands Nelly, naked. Why is that idea so intoxicating? It's a facile, masculine thought. Keeping calm in Nelly's presence, in the presence of the Nelly in the mirror in a young dress, is no doubt within her grasp, and yet she can't control it at her discretion.

"I'm too old for it, but I still get a kick out of trying these things on once in a while. Five years ago, maybe, but now . . ."

"Why five years ago and not now?"

Nelly seems piqued by the question.

"Don't be impertinent, kid."

"I wasn't being impertinent."

"Come on. Out. I'm going to get changed."

"But I wasn't being impertinent."

Suddenly things are tense, and just as abrupt as the good mood the dress initially brought on, the pendulum swings back the other way. Nelly finally turns to her, pausing theatrically. She's still too powerful. Too powerful and larger-than-life. How might she express her love of that face? How might it be described? It lasts only a second, a second in which she feels she loves her and spurns her, both in half measures, both imperfectly, but also feels that something has changed; she suddenly has the courage of a dog or a madman, she's got nothing to lose, actually feels a singular strength from within, like the kind seen in those Chekhov plays her father liked to read—the weak character, the one who puts up with all of the others' selfishness, one strange night, finally takes a stand and *speaks*. She has often silently admired these particular characters, always female, of Chekhov's—good-hearted, close-mouthed, thought-provoking women who all of a sudden rise up, electric, and *accuse* with incontestable authority; she feels that they contain all of life itself, that they tremble with unrivaled independence and freedom, that not even their accusation is resentful, just a perfect execution of justice and order. *I never asked you to love me*, Nelly would reply straightforwardly, and with that simple statement, that would be the end of it. What would Chekhov say to that?

"Why don't you go outside and wait for me there?"

And this time it is she who is enraged by the question. She manages to hold out a few seconds before leaving—her final act of subversion.

"Fine."

She's more upset than she realized but also weaker than she realized. Her hands are shaking a little as she puts on her coat. She doesn't even acknowledge the shop assistant, simply obeys Nelly—she goes outside. The air is colder now than it was, or that's how it feels, and as she walks out, she suddenly considers the possibility of leaving altogether. For a few seconds, that shimmering fantasy beckons—keep walking and leave her there, in that boutique. But of course that, yet again, would amount to a failure on her own part, not Nelly's. She feels a tingling of fear and displeasure. In the last four months, since Papá died, it's been almost constant but not fully articulated, as though she were shielding herself from a thought she doesn't dare to think—she, too, has been a coward; she, too, ran away from him. It's not an entirely unfounded suspicion. Her mind stores it like a tangible object—she, too, tired of his desperate, full-frontal love, a love so like that of a child. And his months in the hospital, those were another strange journey. Thoughts come in flashes, and the body grows accustomed to doing what it must to get through the day, actions do not become more spaced out but, on the contrary, more compressed, days become an inventory of things in the enumerative eyes of the patient, force of will leads the power of recollection wherever it can in order to survive: hands; tongue; hair; chest; transfer of assets; evenings glossed with optimism; respect; hope; physical exhaustion; the inability to speak; the simplicity of a map of life unfolded on the table—*This is where I . . .* All of it necessary. But when it's over (and now it's over, and thank God she wasn't there when it *happened*), there comes something like a visionary insight into the deceased, like a long, seductive line, like the white strip of the horizon on a beach. The deceased (no longer Papá, impossible to keep calling him *Papá*) is as pervasive as a splatter, as electric sparks, he disappears and suddenly reappears here, in full force, on the way out of a boutique, in the cold, he was forgotten and now suddenly barges in as though to demand this: *Don't misinterpret me, don't fabricate me, don't make of me what you need.* It is important to be loyal to the deceased, but it's not that easy, and she's not that strong. While waiting for Nelly and still savoring the possibility of running off and leaving her there (what face would she make?), she recalls Nelly's reactions over the course of those months: *How does he look?* Papá didn't ask Nelly to visit, but he yearned for it. The scope of Papá's yearning was astonishing, the whole fraudulent and frivolous range of motives and, deep down, the knowledge that he would arouse no pity, the assurance that he would produce only disgust and hostility (*Antonio, at least admit that you basically did this to yourself*), but when it comes to yearning, risk doesn't matter. At times it is hateful, that morass of yearning tinged with love. It bursts in without warning, the two press against one another, each inhaling the heat of the other, like a fix, a drug, and she knows that Papá's mind is focused solely on that image, as though his entire will to live were contained within it, a will that, given the circumstances, is now starting to seem unnatural and resemble a tantrum, resemble childishness. How could anyone suspect something so base, so shocking as this: the idea that death itself, in the end, would seem like a tantrum. And yet Nelly—*What does he look like? Is he recognizable?* He looks swollen. *I don't know if I'll go see him. What would be the point, at this stage?* It was eerie, too— Nelly's words betrayed no fear, none of the predictable distress that a dying body produces in a healthy one, none of that aversion, only a feeling of contractual obligation to her own life in the here and now and an utter lack of awareness of the conventional understanding of loyalty. It was actually an authentic reaction—*What would be the point?* But one that does nothing to quell Papá's longing, in fact nourishes it; day after day, he wakes, and she knows that the thought grows in him (*Air out the room a little, it's stuffy, don't you think? Just in case she stops by*).

"Oh, there you are, I didn't see you," says Nelly, coming out of the boutique, holding a bag.

"You bought the dress?"

"I did."

It's an emphatic *I did*, assertive, and seems to convey, *Don't you dare say a word*. She's aged a bit now, she thinks. Now that she's bought the dress, she's aged a bit. This is Nelly's first false step. There must have been others, surely, but this is the first one that she can see clearly, and it alters the temperature on the street a little, alters her own temperature, and her own fear. A minute ago, she was on the verge of storming off, now she's glad she didn't go, so that she can witness the apparently innocuous scene— Nelly's failure on leaving Sybilla with a dress she will never wear, a dress bought for the Nelly that was, not the Nelly that is. When she was seven years old, Nelly gave her the doll she'd wanted when she was six, brought it from London with great fanfare (*You won't believe what's in this bag*); she remembers her spellbound fascination, the needless torture of not being allowed to open it until after lunch, and, on opening it, the sense of vanquished yearning, the object of her desire presented once that desire had been extinguished, the absurd blondeness of the doll insulated in her clear plastic box, the long-gone yearning, and the shame of having been dying at one time for that blonde, sun-kissed doll, a shrunken Veronica Lake. At fifty-six, Nelly has bought the dress she would have wanted at fifty. She's angry with herself and doesn't feel like talking, so it is she who speaks now, instead. The air is heavy with something akin to kindness, and to sadness. Now that she is more pathetic, she loves her more, but it's a

192

detached love. If she could at least turn to her and say, *What an idiot, can you believe it? I actually bought that dress* . . . But she can't, and the fact that Nelly can't speak is an extension of the failure of having bought it, in the same way that her defunct love for the doll penetrated and distended the actual body of the doll she no longer wanted. And that is why she is the one who now speaks, as though this were an act of graciousness, as though this were the only act possible—pretending she doesn't know what's going on. Is that what love is? She has an evil way of being kind. She has an evil way of loving her.

She says, "We could go to Yves Saint Laurent to find something for Aunt Lu."

And, "Look, I think it's starting to clear up."

And, "I love the white light of Madrid."

Nelly nods at almost everything, glances alternately at her and the sky; she, meanwhile, thinks the bag with the dress begins weighing less heavily, becomes gradually lighter and lighter, and, for a moment, becomes almost imperceptible, a phantom weight mysteriously counterbalancing the weight of Madrid. *I don't like games, I don't like people who don't say what they mean,* Nelly often says. And she remembers one time when she returned from a trip to China (*The most frightful country I have ever visited in my life*) and told a story about a pit with the statues of two traitors inside it, statues that had been put there seven hundred years ago, and to this day, when people pass by, they spit in it. *They were shiny, you know? Those statues . . . people had been spitting on them for seven hundred years.* What makes her think of that now? It's like the prickling of an intuition, the fear that scorn might extend beyond the grave, the fear that there's no way to clean the Calle Serrano—which they have now returned to—and no way to clean the hospital sheets, no way to clean her memory. She's done nothing with her life. She is thirty years old and she's done nothing with her life—study business, spend two years living in Paris, take care of Papá, adore Nelly, spurn Nelly, try to live as though Nelly didn't exist, forget about her, even. The secrets, frustrations, and accomplishments of a poor little rich girl, a spoiled child.

Yves Saint Laurent is a bruised and battered world, a stifling world—nothing like the restraint of Loewe or the sensuality of Sybilla—a distended, slightly hostile world, and Aunt Lu is the most difficult of all her aunts to buy for. Nelly deals with it the way she deals with all things difficult: by going with the first thing that pops into her head and reacting with incredulity to any displeasure or disappointment—*I thought it was absolutely perfect for you.* Despite being a fussy person herself, Nelly cannot comprehend the fussiness of others; she is a complicated woman yet finds it absurd that others' needs are not simple. Did that signal a lack of imagination, or selfishness? She's not sure. The annoyance she's sometimes felt at this character trait of Nelly's has dissipated. Sometimes Nelly requires the same sort of patience as a child everyone knows is *sweet,* or rather, not that bright. Or maybe the patience required for a truly *pure* child. And when she shows that kind of patience, out of the blue, she suddenly feels herself slip, and she can see Nelly's face, a face as unfathomable as that of an animal. The store is shockingly vile, as though Yves Saint Laurent's designers had all lost their minds and begun making clothes for government officials' mistresses—tacky, provincial women, old hens strutting around like spring chickens.

This time, she elects to stick with Nelly, to protect herself from her by sticking close. She has the uneasy feeling that words have lost their force. She got that with Papá sometimes, too, as though, more than his daughter, she were his lover. But it was not a silent feeling, in fact quite the opposite; throughout his sickness, she heard a sort of muffled sound, like someone crunching through dry foliage, or rustling a newspaper, a sound older than herself, a sound that had traveled a very long time, entire summer afternoons (Nelly in the summertime—that blue bathing suit of hers), dresses like the one Nelly was now inspecting with a vague look of concentration (or was it displeasure?) in her eyes.

"It's hot in here, isn't it?"

"It is," she replies; like Nelly, she has suddenly started to sweat beneath her coat.

The heat prompts a kind of stupor, and they remove their coats in unison. As she's taking hers off, she notices a woman who walked into the store with them. It's as if something about her is a little off. She looks about forty, she is neither unattractive nor attractive—she has thin, almost washed-out lips void of lipstick; large, slightly startled-looking eyes that dart from side to side with astonishing speed; a big coat she hasn't taken off despite the heat; and the tiny, nervous hands of a bird. *Something is about to happen*, she thinks. And then she's sure—that woman *is about to steal something*. What makes her instinctively press against Nelly?

195

There is something linear, like a chain of cause and effect—the urge to scream, to warn not the storekeepers but Nelly, or the thief herself, maybe. By her appearance, you'd never guess. She continues casually leaning over earrings and necklaces, wanders elsewhere a bit, returns to her original spot, from time to time taking refuge in the to-and-fro of other shoppers, as though using them as a barricade; she seems enveloped in a sort of cloud of dust.

"You're making me *hot*," Nelly says.

"Let's get out of here."

"Have you found anything?"

"No, but there's nothing here I like."

"Me, neither."

Then suddenly it happens, right before they walk out. They put their coats back on, and she sees the woman slip something up her sleeve, she can't tell what; it's an anxious move, extremely agile, like a magician's sleight of hand. Did that just happen or not? What vanished? A pair of earrings, a necklace perhaps? The woman heads toward them, preparing to use them as cover on her way out. She can feel the contact of the woman behind her, almost pressing into Nelly, who hasn't picked up on a thing, and as they reach the door, an employee stops all three of them and then turns straight to the woman.

"Could you come with me for a moment, please?"

"Who? Me?" asks Nelly.

"No, not you. If you don't mind," he says, addressing the woman.

"Why?"

His expression has the mark of a hunter—the triumph, the lack of sensitivity, the contrived courtesy. The woman knows why, he knows why. She suddenly feels absurdly distressed, as though she herself were the thief—the knotted contraction of her throat, the wheeziness of her breath, the sudden pounding of her heart.

"What's going on?" asks Nelly.

"You're free to go, there's nothing to worry about," he responds, but when she turns to the woman, she sees that he's grabbed her wrist, a seemingly banal gesture, almost genteel yet quietly rough, a fact that can be seen immediately in the painful contraction of the woman's face.

"You're hurting me," she whispers.

"Come with me, please."

"I'm in a hurry, what do you want?" she asks in a desperate attempt to flee, continuing forward. His reply is no longer genteel.

"You know perfectly well."

"Would you mind *letting go of her arm*?" Nelly asks, still oblivious to it all. Then it suddenly seems to dawn on her, perhaps upon looking at the woman. The whole scene is absurd, like during the final months of Papá's life when from one moment to the next, in the middle of the most everyday of actions, there would suddenly be violence and shame, a fingering, a recognition of guilt; it's a body language that she can feel as if she were making her way through a dark, unfamiliar room full of furniture and objects she trips over. What a farfetched world, she thinks. Then there comes a desperate look, or that's what she thinks it is, from the woman. And a callous look, or that's what she thinks it is, from Nelly.

"Let's go," she says.

They turn and leave. She looks behind her for the last time to see the shop assistant leading the woman back into the store. Then, instantly, they are outside once more, back in the cold and joy of the snow. It's starting to snow again. It strikes her as odd, the way the world immediately demands obedience to its designs.

"She stole something, didn't she?" Nelly asks.

"I think so."

"But did you see it?"

"I saw her over near the earrings, and then I saw her come over toward us, like she wanted to pretend all three of us were together."

Nelly walks in silence a few seconds, headed who knows where, simply out of nervousness, and she walks beside her. Is she indignant? Furious? It's always the same with Nelly, it's as though even at the most decisive moments, things just brush up against her, but their contact is never more than a light swaying. And she, too, touches her perhaps too lightly, perhaps she, too, is too alarmed to make more definitive contact. Why are they both so upset? *I can't feel sorry for everyone, I don't have time for that,* Nelly has said more than once. *Am I supposed to apologize if my heart doesn't bleed for every poor soul on the planet?* At that moment, an attractive man passes and glances at Nelly with interest, an interest she doesn't even register. She's in her own world. *Cowardice is a skill,* is another thing she says. A mystifying declaration. All at once, she whirls sharply.

"You've never stolen anything before, have you?"

"Who, me?" she asks. Like on a test at school, her reply is intended to buy time, but Nelly takes it as a negation, and then she makes an even odder assertion.

"Women's obsession with stealing *makes me sick*." She says it with real scorn, as though she herself were not a woman, or as though the comment were simply physical and what she can't stand is their smell. The temperature has dropped with the snow yet again, and she can see the warm breath on Nelly's lips. Her words, the words she has just spoken, hang in the air, like her breath, like a hot, damp truth. Women and their qualms about possession. Strange qualms about possession, like hidden defects buried deep in the roots of their flesh, defects that never yield to exhaustion, that are always present: the compulsive urge to possess, the inability to ever possess. Perhaps Nelly is actually—in that one way, despite everything else—more male. She herself, most certainly, is not. She is reckless when it comes to possession, feels it fitfully, as with all things that truly interest her, feels its violent impulse turn on and off, and yes, she most certainly has stolen. What would happen if she told Nelly now, right now, after what she's just said? Her stealing might have been even pettier than the woman in the boutique's, more pernicious. What would happen if she just said, flat out, *I actually stole from you once*? How would Nelly react?

She remembers that Papá was still alive when it happened, that she'd stopped by Nelly's for a visit, that Nelly had gone out and that she knew she wouldn't be back for at least twenty minutes. It's a persistent feeling—she remembers that she's alone and that a strange sense of distress comes over her, that she goes into Nelly's bedroom and opens one of her armoires. This is a forbidden act, an act of abject love. She remembers the feel of the little box where Nelly keeps her costume jewelry, remembers spreading it all out on the bed, bending over it, sitting on her heels. There are pieces she vaguely remembers and others she doesn't recall ever having seen before: a pair of long earrings, a little bracelet, four rings, a black brooch with a white circle in the middle and another, smaller, black circle inside of that. A fixation with the brooch flips on within her like a switch, automatic. She freezes. Could she say that to Nelly—*I froze?* Could she use those words, or would she need other words, vertiginous words, to explain why she felt compelled to put the brooch in her pocket, to wait there as though nothing had happened? Does it make sense to steal what is already hers? Because the brooch both is and is not hers, she is its natural owner, it's hers in the projection of assets, in the already-possessing eyes of a legitimate heir. There has been a breach. Then, when Nelly gets back, she makes a hasty excuse and rushes outside, feeling the unbearable contact of the brooch. She takes it out, holds it in her hand—it's lost its benign splendor but not its weight. Something in her has changed, in her and not in the brooch, it is she who wants to turn around, as though wishing to say to Nelly, *Since you're the one who brought all this on, it's your fault.*

"Nelly . . ."

"Yes?"

"What about you?"

"What about me, what?"

"Have you ever stolen anything?"

Nelly stops suddenly in the middle of the street and turns to her, like an adult preparing to chastise a child. She thinks, *She's going to get mad now.* She thinks *she's going to get mad* as though she were already primed to feel Nelly's violent indignation on her skin. This has happened on other occasions, too, always preceded by the same feeling she has now: a fear like a contagious shiver, the desire to be hated by her mother. Why does she want her mother to hate her? Maybe unconcealed hatred would be a sincere reaction, honest scrutiny, a form of loyalty. She can only be worthy of her love if she is worthy of her hate—a deranged thought, and yet having it there in the middle of the Calle Serrano, beneath the timidly falling snow seems, for some reason, to make it more tolerable.

"Why are you asking?"

"I don't know."

What did she do? What nerve did she touch? She touched off something *by mistake*. She knows, at that moment, she is absolutely certain that she has—something in Nelly seems to quiver, to rattle like a train. And from one second to the next, her expression becomes intense, strange.

"Once. I stole once," she replies. "Satisfied?"

"No."

"End of story."

She has a powerful urge to touch her. Not a hug, not a kiss, not a caress, just a simple touch, and she's about to do it, but then she hesitates, and her reach becomes an awkward, slightly ridiculous lunge, as though she were pretending to trip while standing still. She's never seen Nelly give that look before; it's not a compassionate look, not an ashamed look, not a furious look. There's something detached about it, something calm, something animal, but like a tired animal that looks patronizingly on everything, even its own instincts. She needs to capture that look of Nelly's, needs to devour it and then regurgitate it, to scrutinize it. *She feels nothing,* she thinks. Is that the case now, is that what has, perhaps, always been the case? It would be too simple to think that Nelly feels nothing, but in formulating the thought, there does appear to be an element of truth. To think that Nelly feels nothing is, in fact, the beginning of the true thought, the true concept, it is to put her hand on the doorknob and push the door open, and now she'll walk through that door and see what's in there. *Today will be the day*, she thinks, she's sure, today will be the day, all she has to do is follow the course of that thought the way a lost hiker follows the course of a river.

"I didn't mean to upset you," she says as they both resume walking, but she instantly regrets her words; they don't sound right. Nelly takes no time to react.

"That's exactly what you've been meaning to do since the moment you set eyes on me this morning, kid." There is no trace of reproach in her reply, only, once again, detachment and the sound of Nelly's heels, and her three-quarter-length coat flapping open and closed in its own strange, fascinating language. It's odd—each of Nelly's movements exhibits a peculiar sense of ownership. One time, her father made a surreal comment, when Nelly had left home and she asked him if she was coming back. *She'll come back*, he said, *because we belong to her*. She thinks of that now, too. Silence is not an extension of anger. In fact, anger hasn't even touched Nelly, not really. Silence, instead, is an extension of that assertion that brooks no failure: *She'll come back, because we belong to her.*

After that, they go to the restaurant. The white linen tablecloth, the four glasses all lined up in a row, the glimmering silverware, the menu printed on rough, off-white parchment that is pleasing to the touch, the steady stream of others' conversations. They were both suddenly hungry, so Nelly brought her to a restaurant she liked and that she herself had never been to. There is a marvelous cavalcade of pleasures, a clean, sweet vibe, as though anything said there, any exchange, any conversation, even the most banal, would suddenly be made beautiful, as though in a lovely daze. That's exactly what she feels now, after the uneasy conversation that brought them there—respite, as though all the lovely things in this world had graciously lined up to offer their gifts in compensation. Perhaps it's also Nelly's prudence at not having argued a point that's impossible to resolve. Is there any way to know if people's different qualities are virtues or defects? What seemed like an infuriating defect in Nelly twenty minutes ago is now an extraordinary virtue—her methodical analysis of the menu (*Don't even think of ordering the ravioli, that's the one thing they don't do well here*), her leisurely selection, the fun they have glancing furtively at what the people around them have ordered, the excellent wine, the temporary suspension of Christmas madness that is only noticed now that it's been neutralized. She'd like to ask forgiveness. Ask forgiveness and be grateful. But even more satisfying is to curb that impulse and concentrate instead on the physical: the pleasure of hunger about to be satisfied, the faint aroma of hot bread wafting through the restaurant, her glass of wine. She tastes it with a slow, slightly dramatic fake-expert flourish and nods her approval to the waiter, who smiles.

Customs, we have too few customs, she thinks. Papá liked that quote. Who was it from?

"Customs, we have too few customs," she says aloud, happily, in a singsong, learned-by-heart tone, like a somewhat out-of-place nineteenth-century actress.

"Who said that?"

"Papá."

Nelly gives a shocked smile.

"He did? I never would have thought."

"It's a quote, actually, I can't remember who said it first, he used to say it when he was happy that we were all together."

His private words, private quotes, private thoughts, she knows them, has encountered them many times, has lived with them. At that moment, she sees the subtle, roundabout nature of that quote, which is a tribute to Nelly, like using a third party to let someone else know that they are loved. *What's this business of going around announcing "I love you" all the time? How can anyone have the nerve to say such a thing?* Nelly once said. The deceased retreats slightly, for the first time in four months. She notices but feels no guilt, as though life, and not the deceased, had the delicate, graceful hand; the deceased recedes in the most ordinary of ways: with the arrival, finally, of their food—vegetable lasagna for Nelly, gnocchi in cream sauce for her.

"We still need something for Aunt Lu."

"We'll go to ABC Serrano after this, we'll find something there," Nelly says, aborting the topic.

It is both typical and familiar, this way of avoiding the unpleasant. She concentrates on her lasagna. Nelly never pays attention to anyone when she eats, instead draws herself in like an animal intent only on its own pleasure; her mannerisms become even more refined, a mix of gestures—some instinctual, like a filly, others aristocratic, like an empress. Perhaps, she thinks, bemused, no two things have more in common—a filly and an empress. Now she, too, concentrates—as though imitating Nelly—on her gnocchi, on the fresh, full pleasure of their texture, the way they almost melt in her mouth. She orders more wine. She likes drinking. Sometimes her compulsion to drink is like a nervous tic, and it always happens with wine. Is this reasonable, to suddenly be overflowing with pleasure, feel the first stages of inebriation, rejoice at being alive and being here, at being able to inspect Nelly's face unnoticed, with impunity? Finally, she does—it is a classic face, really. That of an emperor's wife, of Caesar's daughter. Once, in the Museum of Roman Art in Mérida, in one of the halls, she was shocked to note the uncanny resemblance between one of the busts and Nelly's face. It was nothing as simple as *physical* resemblance—though, in fact, there was an element of that, too: the delicate outline of brows and lips, the fullness of cheekbones, mellowing in the cheeks, all coming together in the strong chin—but something more abstract, harder to define: a sort of authority.

"A man once killed himself over me, I think about that a lot," she says out of the blue.

"Excuse me?"

Nelly dabs her lips with her napkin and takes a sip of wine, arranges her blouse. She glances at the waiter and beckons him with a wave.

"Are any of your desserts homemade?"

"The pannacotta, it's excellent."

205

"We'll have one, and two spoons."

She turns back to her, takes out a cigarette. Nelly smokes only during dramatic pauses. Her day-to-day life is full of dramatic pauses, as though she constantly needed to demarcate, to keep the lurching boundaries of things in check.

"A man, a boy, killed himself over me, more than twenty years ago."

Nelly made this announcement and took a long drag on her cigarette, unaffected, indulgent. Nelly's mannerisms at critical moments display a sort of syntax of impersonality, though that's not the case now. She's not nervous, at least not in any realistic way.

"You never told me that before."

"I've never told *anyone* that before."

"What happened?"

"He sent me letters. Followed me. He was the son of some friends of my father's. Said he was in love with me. I can't even remember his face, but I remember that whenever I went out, I was afraid he'd be there. He had this steady, detached expression, blank, a look so empty it was almost the absence of a look. I don't remember his face, but I remember that look. It was *repulsive*."

The waiter arrives with their pannacotta and two gleaming spoons, one beside the other. Nelly smiles her thanks and immediately plucks up one of the spoons. She plays a little with the pannacotta and finally brings a miniscule portion to her mouth.

"Not bad," she proclaims.

She, too, takes a taste. It's true, it's not bad. She'd like to say something, but Nelly doesn't seem to require it. And she doesn't want to lie to herself, either—she feels nothing. Or nothing that might contribute to what Nelly just said. The logical thing to do would be to ask for details, tease out some of the morbid particulars: what, exactly, being followed entailed; how he killed himself; what his name was; whether Nelly saved the letters. The logical thing might be even more pernicious and more absurd—to think that Nelly is the way she is *because of that*. The thought almost makes her laugh. She does feel something, after all: an absolute awareness of how futile it would be to add anything. And something else: despite loving Papá more, she's always sided with Nelly, and that is disconcerting. She's always thought Nelly was the one who was *right*.

When they leave, they head straight for the ABC Serrano shopping center, to find a gift for Aunt Lu. They each walk alone, really, though not distant, not lost in their own thoughts. The temperature has fallen again. She moves in closer, and when she feels the contact of Nelly's overcoat on hers, she slips her arm into Nelly's. The sight of people on the street gives her a strange feeling, as if there were something unbelievable about them, as if they were straightening their knees and trembling, as if, by sheer luck, they'd just been saved from some danger. When she gets like that, she can't help herself, she imagines all those people in bed, having sex, their faces contorted and then satisfied, the touch of their skin, something bristling inside them; it comes out in a pained, nervous expression, inaccessible, but right now there is something strange about the contact of Nelly's arm, it seems to be precisely what is keeping her from those thoughts. At times, the thought of having been born of her is terrifying; now,

207

curiously, it is not. She's always known it and has sometimes used it to her advantage, no doubt in the same way Nelly has used other thoughts about which she knows nothing. But in fact, it is the street that imposes itself on her like a language. Still, she would like to turn to Nelly and say, *I wish you were inside me, I wish I never had to struggle to speak, I wish I could believe that you would remember, that I could entrust myself to you, I know this is a corrected version of the truth, I know that and I try to listen, and in your body and the touch of your coat, I know there is a larger truth.* But attending to that drawn-out thought, here on the Calle Serrano, beneath a once-more disturbingly bright sky, gives her a vertiginous feeling, like she's rushing through the air on a swing in the park.

The ABC Serrano shopping center is soothingly impersonal and mysteriously half-empty. If someone said that she and Nelly were never going to speak again, she'd believe it, because speaking is no longer required, but when Nelly turns to her and says, "How bizarre, don't you think? There's almost no one here," she responds naturally.

"I know, they must all be having lunch still."

Suddenly she is afraid, she doesn't want to think too much, doesn't want to think about Papá, about the boy who killed himself over Nelly. Why does it seem so reasonable, this preposterous idea of killing oneself over Nelly? They browse, moving ghostlike through several shops, make the remaining purchases, gifts for Aunt Lu, for some cousins. Nelly is almost always the one to do it, the one to decide, and she sees Nelly as a constant source of interference that makes her need to distrust both the things she feels and those she has no name for.

What happens next is something she will try to explain several times over the course of her life, without ever succeeding. Every time, this is where she'll start, but leaving out Nelly's earlier confession in the restaurant. She'll say, *We were at a mall, doing some Christmas shopping; my father had died four months earlier.*

And, *suddenly, we came out of a store and there was this commotion, everyone was uneasy, looking up.*

"What's going on?" Nelly asks.

"I don't know."

It's a bird, they spot it almost immediately. But not just any bird.

"What kind of bird is *that?*"

She is awestruck at the bird's beauty. Flapping around the shopping center's small, domed ceiling is an animal the size of a child's torso, with iridescent green, yellow, and red plumage. Its beauty is unquestionable, majestic, all the more majestic for the outlandishness of its present location and the unusual silence it has occasioned. For a second, it is as though there were no yuletide flurry, no canned Christmas carols.

"It's a bird of paradise," someone says.

"What's it doing here?"

She turns to Nelly. She, too, is gazing up at the bird with intense emotion. In the silence, she gets the strange feeling that she can see the veins in her face the way you see veins in a wooden flute. Then she looks back at the bird. It has flown up to the top of the domed ceiling, attempted to fly through it, and collided with the glass. Now it flies down several feet, flapping wildly, and makes a second attempt. This time there is a dull thud, and the bird plummets vertically, as though aflame, onto a third-floor railing. Someone lunges for it. There is a sharp intake of breath. It attempts to take flight once more, this time wearily, losing some of its golden tail feathers. And now it falls to the floor, where it begins a crazed, circular flapping around the food court tables. Several people try to approach it, but the bird takes off again, determined this time, flapping up to the third floor, and from there into the dome once more, this time making no attempt to fly through it. Time is suspended for a moment, majesty renewed, as though it were rising once more. That, too, is something she will attempt to explain, that sort of second dignity of the bird in all its splendor, its flamboyant plumage fanned, and God knows how many other things, things that she may not even have felt at the time but that later filtered through to her memory, the image of the bird like a sieve—Nelly's presence like white noise, like the hum of electricity, the hushed cacophony of Christmas, people's faces flushed from the heat in the mall, their shopping bags heavy with Christmas presents; it all takes on a strange texture again, a melancholy dignity, a perception like the soft buzz of a presence. That's when Nelly says, "It's marvelous."

"What is?"

"That creature. Don't you think it's marvelous?"

"Yes," she responds, without thinking. In fact, she feels vaguely afraid of the bird of paradise, as though there were something captivating yet evil about it, something obscene, something uncontrollable, an aggressive overabundance.

The bird of paradise swerves and lets out a tremendous squawk, attempts to change the course of its flight but stops, flaps up anxiously, vertically, making it eight or ten feet, and then collapsing in a single tremendous crash amid the tables where people had been eating. Everyone recoils, alarmed, as though rather than a bird, it were an Aztec curse befallen them. Someone screams, and then a squawking, green shadow begins to run and flap like a chicken through people's legs. It runs back and forth, its squawks becoming shriller, and at that moment, certain it's headed for them, she instinctively draws back. This, too, is something she will recall: she grabs Nelly's arm as though trying to protect her, and Nelly doesn't move. What's more, there is something unnatural about how rigid Nelly stands, as though she's been seized by something. The bird of paradise flaps distractedly toward where they stand and passes with a ruffling of wings and a strange, acidic, animal smell. Then it stops in a corner and retucks its wings. It's like a deranged grande dame with crazed eyes, unnaturally widened eyes.

She recalls every move: the way Nelly bends down to deposit the shopping bags on the floor and then straightens, slowly, silently, with great care, a care she's never seen in her before, will never see again; the way she approaches the bird firmly but at a glacial pace; the way she reaches it and leans over, as though absorbed in silent observation; the way she places a hand on the bird of paradise's puffed-up chest; and the subtle way the bird responds, with an almost imperceptible shudder, and then submits. Nelly begins to stroke it, but there is nothing sensual in her touch, just something that seems to howl like the wind or shriek like a child. And then she has an unflinching, impossible thought—*How will Nelly die, when she dies?*

ABOUT THE AUTHOR

ANDRÉS BARBA MUÑIZ (MADRID, 1975) is a Spanish novelist, essayist, translator, scriptwriter and photographer. He is the author of a total of twelve books of literary fiction, non-fiction, photography, art and children's literature. He has been awarded numerous prizes, including the Premio Torrente Ballester de Narrativa (for *Versiones de Teresa*), the Premio Anagrama de Ensayo (for *La ceremonia del porno*) and the Premio Juan March de Narrativa (for *Muerte de un caballo*). He was also shortlisted in the XIX Premio Herralde de Novela (for *La hermana de Katia*, made into a film a few years after by Mijke de Jong). In 2010 he was featured in Granta's magazine as one of the twenty-two best young Spanish-language writers. His works have been translated into ten languages.

ABOUT THE TRANSLATOR

LISA DILLMAN translates from the Spanish and Catalan and teaches at Emory University in Atlanta. Some of her recent translations include *The Mule*, by Juan Eslava Galán, *Me, Who Dove Into the Heart of the World*, by Sabina Berman, and Christopher Domínguez Michael's *Critical Dictionary of Mexican Literature*. She's currently translating Yuri Herrera's *The Transmigration of Bodies*.

CPSIA information can be obtained
at www.ICGtesting.com
Printed in the USA
FFOW02n2009031114
8433FF